Mansion of Smiling Masks

Mansion of Smiling Masks

Daoma Winston

Thorndike Press **Chivers Press**
Thorndike, Maine USA • **Bath, Avon, England**

This Large Print edition is published by Thorndike Press, USA and by Chivers Press, England.

Published in 1994 in the U.S. by arrangement with Jay Garon Brooke Associates, Inc.

Published 1994 in the U.K. by arrangement with Judy Piatkus (Publishers) Ltd.

U.S.   Hardcover   0-7862-0216-5 (Romance Series Edition)
U.K.   Hardcover   0-7451-2368-6 (Chivers Edition)
U.K.   Softcover   0-7451-2384-8 (Camden Edition)

The text of this Large Print edition is unabridged.
Other aspects of the book may vary from the original edition.

Set in 16 pt. News Plantin by Penny Picard.

Printed in the United States on acid-free paper.

British Library Cataloguing in Publication Data available

Library of Congress Cataloging in Publication Data

Winston, Daoma, 1922–
      Mansion of smiling masks / Daoma Winston.
         p.   cm.
      ISBN 0-7862-0216-5 (alk. paper : lg. print)
      1. Large type books. I. Title.
      [PS3545.I7612M36   1994]
      813'.54—dc20
                                                        94-9230

For Murray

Chapter 1

The vibrations seemed to ripple through Mari like small shivers of fear, and she, thinking uneasily ahead to when the plane would land, moved closer to Leigh.

She rubbed her cheek against his jacket, enjoying the feel of the silken fabric, and beneath it, the hard, corded curve of his shoulder. But more important, there was the comforting reassurance that she was actually with him. She did not like to think of how it might have been. Leigh, on his way home, alone, and she left to wait in the old apartment with Susie, commiserating but smug.

Still, Mari hoped that she had been right in her desperate pleas to be allowed to join Leigh. There was so much she didn't know, didn't understand.

Through the screen of her heavy lashes, she studied his angular profile. Then, quickly, as if she were using pen and ink, but in her mind, she sketched him full face as she had first seen him.

His hair was dark, close-cropped. His eyes were dark, too, brown, but set deep, and with shadows that often seemed to turn them black. Above them, his heavy brows made the skeptical lines that formed his expression. His mouth was skeptical, too, the lips firm and thin, and sad in repose.

She wished that he would look down at her and smile. She had learned, in the five weeks she had known him, that when he smiled a glow came into his face, a warm, earthy quality which rose up to melt cynicism away. Then, instead of looking older than his twenty-eight years, he seemed younger, softer, more giving. He looked like the man he must have been before tragedy touched him.

She sighed. If only she knew . . . if only she understood. All she wanted was to make him happy, to wipe away forever the memories which marked him. The memories which, in the brief three weeks of their marriage, she had realized hung like threatening clouds on the horizons of their happiness, even though until the day before she had not known their source.

But Leigh did not look down at her and smile.

She understood that he too must be thinking ahead, must be concerned about his grandfather, Judge Sam Douglass.

At her insistence, Leigh had described the household which he had left two years before.

To Mari, who had no family, the number alone was imposing. Besides Judge Sam, who ruled the Douglass family in the patriarchal manner of an earlier era, there were his two elderly daughters, Arlene and Phoebe. There was also Leigh's mother, Amantha, and his thirty-year-old brother, Jeff, who was married to Geraldine. With them lived Fern Carrier, a distant cousin, brought to Douglass Acres as a child by Judge Sam.

Meeting so many people at once, Mari thought, was cause enough for apprehension, if one were hoping for acceptance, even hoping for love.

But that very natural fear was worsened by her knowledge that she would stand in another woman's shadow.

It was to lay that shadow to rest forever that she had begged Leigh to allow her to return home with him.

The small plane lurched, tilted forward.

Instantly, Mari pictured a great diving flame, and spinning fragments, and the earth rising in steamy, mushroom-shaped clouds.

To banish the frightening thought, one more sign of that unbridled imagination which had been her joy, and her problem too, for as long as she could remember, she yawned and straightened up.

"You were so still," Leigh said. "I thought

you were sleeping."

"Resting. Thinking," she told him. Then, "Are we almost there?"

He nodded. "Do up your safety belt."

She fumbled with it until he took the clasp from her clumsy fingers, and hooked it for her. She thanked him, letting her wide smile tell him without words how wonderful it was for her, who had never known it before, to have someone care.

"I hope we find your grandfather better," she said.

Leigh didn't answer.

It was one more sign of his obvious reluctance to talk about his family, his home.

Not wanting to, but unable to stop herself, she asked, "You're not sorry I came with you, are you, Leigh?"

He grinned, and the sadness fell away from his lips. "No, Mari, I'm not sorry."

And Mari, thinking of the shadow of that woman, whose name she didn't know, whose face she couldn't imagine, vowed that he never would be.

The plane lurched again, vibrations stronger, so that small creaks and groans seemed amplified.

She leaned forward to press her face to the window. On the silver wing, outlined by a circle of jagged black lightning, big red print advertised the Red Eagle Charter Service.

Leigh had rented the plane less than an hour before in Boston, and they had flown west, continuing the long journey begun in Copenhagen. Soon they would land near Jessup, and in a little while, she would see Leigh's home for the first time.

She tried to picture it, but for once, her facile imagination failed her. Leigh had said that Douglass Acres was big and old, and hardly more than that.

Dizzying reflections streaked on the wing tips by the brilliant sun caught her attention. Beyond them, the endless sky seemed to be a closed bell of perfect blue. White waves of rolling clouds, as thick as ocean spume, hung below them.

Mari gasped as the plane swooped into the mists. For long, throbbing moments, she was blinded by intense, refracted light. Then, as they emerged into a thin gray overcast, she wondered why the sun had disappeared.

The field was a tiny, dusty strip surrounded, like a stain on a rumpled blanket, by low green hills.

The plane's wheels touched ground, bumped, and rolled to a quick stop.

"It won't be long now," Mari said, smiling.

Leigh rose, and stretched.

The pilot came back to open the doors.

"Any time you're ready," he told Leigh, "just give me a call and I'll fly in and pick you up."

"It won't be more than a few days," Leigh answered. To Mari, he added, "I hope."

He leaped to the ground, then swung her down beside him.

The pilot tossed out the luggage, waved, and slammed the door shut.

The field was empty except for a ramshackle building that stood yards away near the road.

Leigh nodded toward it, picking up the bags. "I'll phone the grocery store in town. Old Ned there can send a cab for us."

She hurried to keep up with him, clutching her coat, wondering if her gloves were in her purse, and struck with surprise, said, "There's nothing here, Leigh."

"A far cry from Kennedy Airport," he agreed.

Left alone when he went into the shack to make the call, she thought that it was a far cry from anywhere she had ever been.

There was, first of all, the singular emptiness. Not a house in view, not a car, not a soul in the fields. Except for the graveled road, the unpainted wall against which she leaned, it might have been a place undiscovered by man.

And then there was the strange light. The

brilliant sun and the blue sky of the higher altitudes were hidden by a layer of clouds the color of oil smoke that hung, brooding, over the hills, and cast a pall of yellow-gray on the rolling meadows. Her painter's eyes considered it with disapproval. It was an unattractive color, somehow unclean, unhealthy.

Her skin seemed to prickle. Her face grew stiff. The warm, damp air on the June afternoon was difficult to breathe.

Her earlier apprehension flowered into fear. Suppose she could not lay to rest the shadow of the woman who haunted Leigh? Suppose she had been wrong in coming to Douglass Acres?

And why, why had Leigh been so reluctant to have her with him?

A gust of wind caught her skirt as the small plane taxied down the field, passed her by.

She turned to watch its bumpy start, and to follow its sudden easy glide into the air.

In another few days, she thought, it would return for her and Leigh. They would pick up their lives again. In Copenhagen, Amsterdam, wherever he wanted to go. It didn't matter to her. As long as they could be together. The wonder that he had chosen her wrapped her in a curious warmth.

Women always looked at him, noticed his height, the width of his shoulders, the hook

13

of skepticism in his dark brows.

And Mari knew herself well. She was small, only a little over five feet tall, and very slender. She looked much younger than her age, which was twenty-two. Her thick short hair was a clear gold, and clung to her head in a gleaming cap. The tiny bangs over her round brow stressed her faintly tilted, almond-shaped eyes, and seemed to reflect shifting golden lights in their tan depths. Her cheekbones were high, her nose small and straight, her lips full, vulnerable to hurt. She wore a simple white silk shirt, with a strand of pearls at her throat, and a narrow black skirt.

She knew that she was attractive, but she knew, too, that she didn't have the dash, the élan, which gave a woman true distinction. Until she had met Leigh, she hadn't cared.

He, suddenly at her elbow, said, "It won't be more than a few minutes." Then, "You're watching the plane go as if you wish you were on it."

"Oh, no," she laughed.

"I do," he told her soberly.

She didn't know what to say, so she didn't answer.

He went on, "The man coming for us will probably be Jonah Grimes. He's our housekeeper's brother. Her name is Nellie, and without her, I imagine that Douglass Acres might just fall down."

Leigh lit a cigarette then, and by the time it was finished, and ground into the dust, the cab pulled up.

A small man, lean and wizened as a jockey, jumped out. He wore blue jeans, a black and red checked shirt, and a peaked cap. He bounded around the cab, poked Leigh's arm lightly, and grinned. "Ned thought it was you on the phone. Only Nellie never told me you were coming, so I didn't believe his old ears."

"Nellie probably didn't know," Leigh said. "I didn't wire to say when I'd be arriving."

Jonah put the bags into the trunk. "Okay, you two, get in. You've come a long way, haven't you?"

"A very long way," Leigh said. Then, "Jonah, how's Judge Sam?"

"About the same." When they were in the cab, and under way, Jonah went on, "You home for good now?" His sharp blue eyes studied Mari's reflection in the mirror.

"Just for a few days. I came to see Judge Sam." Leigh paused, then grinned suddenly, "I suppose I ought to get you off the hook. So I'll tell you this is Mari, my wife."

"Well, I figured," Jonah laughed. "I'm not so dumb as all that, am I? And Nellie's talked of nothing else since they got your letter a

15

couple of weeks ago."

Mari, touching the plain gold band on her finger for luck, smiled at him, and he smiled back in obvious approval.

The cab was moving into the rolling hills by then. Pine and blue spruce and hemlock spilled long dark streaks across the winding road. Tiny ponds glittered like chips of glass from shallow basins.

Mari decided that as soon as she could she would set up her palette, and paint. She would do the crooked trees, the burned-out fields. She would conquer the brooding countryside by learning to love it. Because it was from here that Leigh had come.

He touched her cheek. "You're very quiet."

"There's a lot to look at."

"Never been here before, have you?" Jonah asked.

"Never," Mari answered. "It's all new to me. All strange . . ." Her voice imperceptibly dropped on the last word, becoming almost a whisper.

"And you, Leigh? How long since you've been home now? A little less than two years, isn't it?"

"That's right," Leigh said.

"And you've been traveling all that time?"

"Yes," Leigh answered.

"Well, I hope it helped you." Jonah's eyes

moved to Mari's reflection again. "And I guess it did."

Mari looked helplessly at Leigh, wishing she could say something quickly to cover the innuendo in Jonah's words. But her mind seemed as blank as the brooding landscape.

Then the cab rounded a curve. Leigh leaned forward. "Jessup," he said in a quiet tone.

It was a small town, just a few blocks of old red brick and stone houses leaning together among dusty storefronts and gasoline stations.

A big brown dog lay in the road. Jonah cut speed, swore softly, blew his horn. The dog, at what seemed to be the last possible safe moment, rose leisurely, stretched, and ambled away.

"There's obviously not much doing," Leigh said.

"June doldrums," Jonah told him. "And it's the same the rest of the year. The young people go, and they don't come back. Why should they? There's nothing for them here."

"What about at Douglass Acres?"

"The same there, too. Of course, one thing is new. Ian Storer hangs around a lot. Courting Fern, they say."

"Do they?"

Ian Storer. It was a name Mari had never heard before, but she knew she would remember it when she saw the suddenly grim look around Leigh's mouth. She put her hand on his, but he didn't seem to notice.

Jonah went on, "Your brother, Jeff, he took the money your father left him and put it into foreign cars. That's what he wanted all his life, I guess. So he finally did it. And went broke last year. Nobody in Jessup buys cars. So he didn't really have a chance, not from the beginning. He should have gone further afield, but I suppose he couldn't do that."

"And what's he doing now?" Leigh asked.

"You know what he's doing."

"The others?"

Jonah shrugged. "Nobody changes much. Geraldine nags, and Arlene and Phoebe stick pretty close to their television." He was silent for a moment. Then, grinning, he added, "At least one good thing. Nobody's seen Old Dandy."

Bewildered, Mari turned to look questioningly at Leigh.

Jonah, probably reading her expression, demanded, "Didn't he ever tell you about Old Dandy?"

"There's some nonsense best forgotten," Leigh said curtly.

"Maybe," Jonah agreed. "Only how are you going to make people forget what they just happen to remember?"

Leigh didn't answer him, nor did he answer Mari's exasperated "But who *is* Old Dandy?"

The cab swung between white stone walls, past a tall iron gate, and into a curved driveway.

Leigh stiffened. "There, Mari. Douglass Acres."

And she, looking past the white blossoms of the horse chestnut trees, was suddenly breathless.

Surrounded by lush, well-tended greenery, the huge mansion dominated the brow of the hill. It was three stories high, and capped by a pitched roof of slate the same color as the gray clouds that seemed to cluster over it. Its red brick had aged to a warm smudged rose, and was undecorated except by the white trim of big empty windows and anchored shutters. The white portico and columns at its front seemed strangely out of place in the New England countryside.

"Leigh," she said at last, "you didn't prepare me for this."

He didn't answer, but Jonah laughed. "I tell you, nobody sees Douglass Acres for the first time without reacting."

He drew up under the portico and stopped.

Mari brushed at her bangs, snatched a compact from her purse and dabbed powder on her nose.

19

"Don't fuss," Jonah told her, his wizened face alight with a grin. "You'll do. You're fine. There's nothing to worry about."

She smiled at him gratefully as he got out, went around to the trunk for the bags.

Leigh, staring silently at the house, sighed, then turned and touched her cheek. "We're here, Mari."

She smiled at him, filled with delight at his gentle gesture. Yet she wondered if he had been thinking of the woman he had once known, lived with, loved in Douglass Acres.

He slowly opened the door, just as slowly climbed out.

Mari saw dread in his dark shadowed eyes.

She took a quick, deep breath, followed him, clutching her coat and purse, thinking of her gloves, but deciding not to forage for them at that moment.

Leigh paid Jonah, spoke a few words to him. Then Jonah got into his cab, waved at Mari, grinned. "Well, good luck," he called and drove away.

As Leigh turned toward the house, the big white door opened.

A tall man, blond, stout, wavering on his feet, stood there, staring. And then he came down the marble steps, rubbing his eyes in a pantomime of disbelief.

"Hello, Jeff," Leigh said.

Mari, watching, instantly sensed Leigh's tension, withdrawal. She wondered why he had responded that way to his brother.

"So the prodigal returns," Jeff cried. "He has found his way home at last."

"I got your cable," Leigh told him in a low hard voice. "I came as fast as I could. How's Judge Sam?"

"My cable? How's Judge Sam?" Jeff frowned, looked bewildered at the same time. "What the hell are you talking about? What cable?"

"The one you sent me saying Judge Sam is ill, and wanted me to come right away," Leigh said more gently, obviously trying for patience. "Come on, Jeff, you know what I mean. You haven't forgotten sending it to me, have you?"

"I haven't forgotten. I just never did it." Jeff wavered on his feet. "I tell you what. If there was a cable really, suppose you let me see it. Suppose you show it to me, huh?"

Leigh stared into his brother's flushed face, then shrugged. "I'm afraid I don't have it, Jeff. Don't you believe me?"

"Sure I believe you. Only how do I know there was one?" Jeff demanded. "You explain it, huh? How do I know?" He paused, wavered in a half circle, to stare at Mari.

There was a joyful shout from the open

21

doorway. A tall, slim girl stood there. She had long dark hair bound back by a braided red ribbon, and a white oval face from which big gray shining eyes and a slashing red mouth seemed to cry for attention. She wore pale blue trousers, a shirt that matched them.

Mari heard Leigh's involuntary exclamation, half gasp, half cry. She put her hand on his arm.

But he shook her reassuring touch away. He raised his head. "Fern," he said "It's you, Fern."

She leaped the steps, flung herself into his arms. "Oh, Leigh, it's wonderful to have you home again."

For a moment, Mari was lost in the rapid cross-talk.

Leigh said, "Fern, you're thinner, you look taller. You've let your hair grow."

"Yes," she said, glowing. "Oh, yes, you noticed, Leigh."

And then Jeff cut in, his bloodshot eyes suddenly full of comprehension. "Hey, Leigh," he yelled, "this is your new wife, isn't it? Well, why don't you introduce us, hah? Why don't you let us welcome her to the ever-loving family?" He sagged against a white column, his flushed face twisted into a grimace, his thick chest heaving with wild laughter.

22

Mari, shrinking back, looked at Leigh for reassurance, and saw the sudden stony set to his mouth, the grooves cut into his cheeks, the new lines graven in his brow.

Chapter 2

Time seemed to stop. It hung breathless, waiting, holding Jeff's words, his wild laughter, alive and echoing in the still air.

Fern was frozen in Leigh's arms.

Leigh himself was a helpless puppet, dangling from broken strings.

Mari felt miles away instead of inches, felt separated from him, as though suddenly a thick layer of glass had descended between them from beyond which her frightened whispers could not be heard.

Then Fern spun away from Leigh. She grabbed Jeff's shoulder, shook him hard. "Stop that," she cried. "Stop that this instant, you fool." And, raising her voice, "Geraldine, come and get this drunken husband of yours. Come get him, I say!"

But Jeff, still roaring with laughter, pulled himself away from Fern and stumbled up the steps, disappearing into the shadows beyond the doorway.

Fern shrugged, turned back to Leigh and Mari, dividing her bright, apologetic smile between them. "Don't pay any attention to him. He hardly knows what he's doing. It's terrible to know you're second best, and always will be, and can't ever hope to be first."

"He doesn't try to be anything at all," Leigh said hoarsely. But then, turning to Mari, he took her hand and introduced her to Fern.

Mari murmured a brief greeting, her lips cold and stiff, her ears still ringing with the ugly sound of Jeff's laughter, her mind still hearing repeated Leigh's hoarse exclamation when he had first looked up at Fern.

"Welcome to Douglass Acres," Fern said. "And please, Mari, dear, do forgive us, if you can, for our small sins." She turned swiftly to Leigh. "Isn't she lovely? And blonde, Leigh. Hair like a golden helmet. Those amber eyes, so young, so wide, so . . . dreaming."

Mari, listening to the cold brittle voice discuss her, appraise her, as if she were invisible, felt herself shrink to conform to the image sketched. She was a small, blonde doll, not real, not alive . . . She forced her suggestible muscles to tighten. She stood tall, smiling. She took Leigh's hand.

"You are back for good, Leigh, aren't you?" Fern asked. "We *do* need you so. We *need* you, Leigh."

"Let's go in," Leigh answered, picking up the bags.

Fern said, shaking back her long dark hair, "Listen, Leigh, I better tell you. Ian Storer will be here for dinner tonight. I hope you don't mind. He and I . . ."

"It's all right," Leigh said tightly.

"If I'd known, Leigh . . . But we hadn't heard . . . and Ian's been so very good . . ."

"It's all right," Leigh repeated.

Mari asked herself who Ian Storer was. Why did his name bring that grim look to Leigh's mouth? Why need Fern apologize for his presence?

She couldn't ask aloud. No one explained.

Leigh led her up the white marble steps.

The hallway was big, dim. The walls were pale gray, a perfect match to the thick carpet. Tapestries and old photographs were hung from floor to high ceiling in irregular patterns. A vast chandelier, shaped like a wagon wheel, with flame-shaped bulbs, hung from an old beam.

Mari eyed the tapestries and photographs with interest, but she had no time to pause to examine them closely.

From somewhere up the wide flight of stairs, there was the sound of Jeff's voice, rumbled words mixed with continuing waves of raucous laughter.

Fern groaned, "Oh, he's impossible. You can see what I mean, can't you, Leigh?"

26

Mari, looking past Fern's shoulder, saw the wide doors beyond slowly open. A woman stood there. Mari knew her instantly. She had Leigh's angular features, but her eyes were a pale blue, matching the tiny sapphire earrings she wore. Her hair was white, carefully waved into a perfect chignon. She wore her blue linen dress as if it were a queenly robe.

Leigh dropped the bags he had been carrying. He grinned, and suddenly his face was alive again. "Amantha, you get younger every day."

"I'm fifty-five years older, and look worse," she said tartly. Then, smiling, she opened her arms. "How wonderful to have you home at last. You can't imagine how much we need you, Leigh. You've seen Jeff, perhaps that explains . . . and there was no reason for you to go, none at all." She raised a delicately rouged, carefully powdered cheek. "But never mind, dear. Never mind all that now."

His grin died, fading slowly, the light in his face fading with it. He bent to kiss her. When he drew away, he said, "I came because of Judge Sam. Where is he? How is he?"

"Where?" Amantha's brows rose in twin arches of question. "Where? Upstairs. Where else?" Then she paused. "Oh dear, I forgot. You didn't know, did you? He doesn't come down any more. He hasn't since you went

27

away. When we want to see him — we have to go up, beg for a moment."

"But is he all right?"

Amantha laughed. "As all right as he ever was. But, perhaps, since your father died . . ." She sighed. "Oh, I don't know, Leigh. I don't know."

Leigh, as if suddenly remembering Mari, took her hand in his cold fingers. He drew her close to him. "This is my wife, Amantha. Mari, my mother."

"I'm happy to meet you," Mari said, speaking slowly, softly, past a sudden lump in her throat.

But time once again seemed to come to a complete stop.

Pale light streaked the pewter candlestick on the shining mahogany table against the wall, caught up the colors of the tapestries, and etched shadows in Amantha's sparkling eyes.

There was another presence in the hallway, a pale breathing presence. The shadow of an unknown woman, gone now, but not forgotten, never forgotten . . .

Mari waited, trembling, for some sign, some small gesture of welcome, while Amantha's blue eyes studied her, empty as shuttered windows.

At last time moved forward again.

Amantha smiled, said softly, "My dear, how wonderful! We were so happy when we heard the news, and we are so happy to have you here." She held out her hands to Mari, hands white and soft as silk, and drew Mari close to her. "It's been my dream, my dream, my dear."

"Thank you," Mari murmured, sensing that the shadow of the unknown woman still lingered, and wondering if, when Amantha looked at her, at Mari, she saw instead that other woman's face.

"I thank *you*," Amantha answered, still smiling the bright smile that didn't warm her eyes. Then, briskly, she went on, "Now. What shall we do? We aren't prepared, of course. You ought to have warned us, to have written, Leigh."

"There wasn't time, Amantha. We started out as soon as possible after we got the cable."

"Cable?"

"I had a cable saying Judge Sam was ill. It was signed with Jeff's name. He claims he doesn't know anything about it."

"I don't understand. Judge Sam's not ill."

"So I've gathered." There was a hard edge in Leigh's voice.

Fern, leaning on the banister, spoke up. "Oh, what difference does it make? You're here, Leigh. That's what counts." She added

29

with a sidelong glance at Mari, "And we've met Mari."

"I don't understand," Amantha repeated. Then she shrugged. "When Jeff is . . . Oh, well, it can't be helped, Leigh." She stopped. "But you will stay, of course. Now that you *are* here . . ."

"For just a few days."

Her brows rose, again in their perfect curves. "But, Leigh . . ."

Fern cut in, "There's only your old room, Leigh. And the help is off on Saturdays as always. But of course, I could run up, and . . ."

"It doesn't matter," Leigh said.

"It doesn't matter," Amantha echoed, with a glance at Mari.

Fern went on, "Then you'll want to go up."

"I think I'd better see Judge Sam right now."

"Good heavens, Leigh. Mari must be exhausted. And you look tired yourself. At least have a rest and a wash, get your land legs," Fern insisted.

Leigh looked down at Mari, looked at her directly for the first time since he had led her up the white marble steps. "Yes, Fern, I suppose you're right." Then, smiling at Mari, "You *do* look a bit tired, darling. Let's get settled first."

30

Amantha, retiring through the draped double doors, said, "The routine is the same,
Leigh. We still get together at four-thirty for
tea in the drawing room. Please do come. It
will give Mari the opportunity to meet the
family." To Mari, she added, "We must have
a long talk, my dear."

Fern put an impulsive hand on Mari's arm.
"If I can help you, just ask me."

Mari thanked her gratefully, hoping that she
had found a friend in Douglass Acres. Perhaps
Fern, who was only a year or two younger
than Leigh, *would* help Mari. Fern had grown
up with Leigh, been like a sister to him. She
would know. She would remember . . .

"We'll be down in a little while," Mari told
her.

Fern nodded, then told Leigh, "I'm sorry
about the room. But Judge Sam keeps Nellie
hopping these days."

Leigh took up the luggage. "Mari?"

She climbed the heavily carpeted stairs,
looking ahead into the shadows of the dim
upper hallway. There was another huge round
chandelier with unlit bulbs shaped like candle
flames.

"To the right," Leigh said, when they had
reached the second floor.

She turned, paused. The stairs continued
up from a square landing. A small alcove, with

31

writing desk and chair, caught her eye.

"That's nice," she said.

"Old houses have all sorts of nooks and crannies."

"And candlesticks, I see." She nodded at the pewter candlestick on the desk. "A twin of the one downstairs, Leigh."

"They're in almost every room in the house. One of the ancestors collected them. In job lots, it would appear."

There was an odd note in his voice. It made her ask, "Don't you like them?"

"I neither like nor dislike them." He nodded. "That way, Mari."

But before she could move, the dim hallway, a moment before full of hushed silence, suddenly throbbed with a long, harsh scream, and a whisper of trembling music.

"What on earth?" Mari gasped.

But Leigh laughed softly. "My aunts. Phoebe and Arlene are at the television set again."

Mari clutched her coat to her. "But it sounded so *real*. It sounded right *here!*"

"They have a suite at the other end of the hall. And they play full volume."

The scream, the music, faded away. "And now for the local news," a voice said in soft and mellow accents.

Mari sighed. "I suppose you do get used

to it after a while."

"You do," Leigh assured her. He went ahead of her then, past a dark green velour settee, a marble-top table on which stood another pewter candlestick. He stopped, nodded, "That's it, Mari," he said expressionlessly.

Mari opened the door for him, went in first, saying, to cover her nervousness, "It's a lovely house, Leigh. Somehow, I never dreamed it would be like this."

"I told you the family had money."

"Yes, but I didn't understand. How would I know? It's a beautiful house, Leigh. And so full of beautiful things. Old, old things. You know, I never cared about that specially. I mean, antiques, not for what they represent. Why admire something just because it's old? I only admire what's beautiful, well made, well kept, useful." She stopped, waited for Leigh to answer her.

But he stood silently in the doorway behind her.

She turned to look at him.

He was hunched, almost bent over, as if the bags he held had suddenly become too heavy for his strength. His tanned face had paled. Even his lips were white. He looked like a man suddenly confronted by the living shape of a nightmare.

She whispered, "Leigh, Leigh, what's wrong?"

But even as she spoke, she understood. This was the house of memory, and this the room. Here he had lived with, loved, the woman he had known before Mari.

Was he thinking of that unknown woman now? Was he remembering her name? Her face? Was he wishing that she, instead of Mari, stood there with him?

"It's all right," he said, with obvious effort. "I think I was just surprised to see it all the same." He set down the bags, went to the window, and drew back the tan drapes. "Yes, it's all the same."

She followed him, leaned against him, seeking the reassurance of his nearness.

The room faced the back of the property. Below them were the two wings that formed an open courtyard which sloped downward in a series of rock garden terraces. The meadows began at the edge of the court and stretched, still and empty, to the yellow-gray hills on the horizon.

She turned away from the view to study the room. It was very large, high-ceilinged. The twin beds were covered by tan and brown spreads; the thick carpet was a warm brown. A huge fireplace, obviously well used, but very clean, took up the greater part of one

34

wall. On its mantel there were two more of the pewter candlesticks which she had come to think of as the symbol of Douglass Acres. A deep leather chair, polished dark brown, was drawn up before the hearth. A small table, with ashtray and pipe, stood nearby. Along the other wall, there were books in shelves, two chests, a small, mirrored dressing-table.

The furnishings were pleasant, luxurious, well tended. Yet the room was peculiarly impersonal, as if no one had ever stayed there long enough to leave his mark. There were no pictures to soften the austere lines of the tan wallpaper, no knickknacks to brighten the wooden surfaces of the chests.

She thought of the sketches in her portfolio. If she chose well, hung a few carefully, the whole quality of the room would be different. It would be less grim, less oppressive.

"I'm going to put up a few of my own little scenes," she told Leigh. "You don't mind?"

"For a couple of days, darling?"

"Why not? Even for a few minutes, Leigh."

"Wherever you are, you make your nest, don't you?"

"I've had to," she said "Like a snail, carrying her house on her back."

He smiled at that, but his eyes, shadowed black, went past her hopeful face, to examine the room.

"Home," he said softly. "I always wondered what it would be like. To come back, to be here again."

She nodded.

"Jeff obviously didn't send the cable, Mari."

"But who could have, Leigh?"

"I don't know. I'll have to find out."

"At least your grandfather's not ill."

"It seems not." There was a harsh edge in Leigh's voice. "I don't like it, Mari."

"But why would anybody do such a thing?"

More gently, he said, "We'll see. But don't you worry your head about it, Mari." He stroked her cheek, then drew away. "We might as well get unpacked, and rest. In a little while, you'll have to face the ordeal by family."

"*I'll* have to?" she demanded.

"I'm going up to see my grandfather. The sooner I understand what's going on, the sooner we get out of here."

"Is it so awful for you, Leigh? So awful to have to remember?"

He didn't answer. He set the bags on the beds, flung his case open, began to unpack.

She watched him for a moment. Then, realizing that she still clutched her coat to her, she looked around for a closet.

There were two doors, one at each end of the far wall. She went to the nearest one, then

36

turned back, her hand on the knob. "Shall I use this one, Leigh?"

He straightened up, stared at her, his eyes blank, his mouth stony. "No," he said harshly. "No, don't touch that door. Don't open it. Not ever."

He lurched to her, knocked her hand away from the knob. He stood over her, looking down into her face.

But he didn't seem to see *her*, Mari thought, frightened, not understanding. He wasn't looking at *her*.

"Why mustn't I use it, Leigh?" she asked softly.

But he shook his head. He strode across the room, seized the small mirrored dressing-table, and half carrying it, half dragging it, he brought it back with him, shoved it in front of the closet door.

"There," he said finally. "That's how it should be, Mari. Shut up. Shut up for good."

Chapter 3

Mari turned her back on the murmuring voices when she heard the sound of the car. It had stopped just below the window. Leigh was at the wheel.

She watched him, hoping that he would raise his eyes to her, that he would look up and smile in the old way. But he stared straight ahead, into an emptiness she couldn't fathom, the new lines graven deeply in his face.

Her fingertips trembled to touch him, to reach down through the open window, past the motionless white roses, to touch him, and with love's warmth to melt the frozen set of his mouth.

She would have believed that only long tormenting years could scar a man so. But she had seen it happen before her eyes.

Now, in an instant of bitter recognition, she knew that she, hopeful as she had been, had somehow failed. Even her love couldn't protect him from the shadows of the past that haunted him always, and that here, in his home, had completely engulfed him.

"Don't look so sad," Phoebe Douglass said,

coming to stand beside Mari. "He's only going into Jessup. Four miles and maybe twenty minutes round trip. He's not going away forever, Mari."

Mari had, only a little while before, met the rest of the family. Now they were all assembled in the big drawing room. Amantha, Fern, Geraldine, Arlene, Phoebe.

Phoebe, very fat, with straight white hair pulled into a knot atop her head, and cookie crumbs on her mouth, gave a faint smile. "My father wants to see Henley Dunroden. He's our attorney. What Judge Sam wants, Judge Sam gets. So Leigh's gone off to collect Henley." Phoebe had a high, sweet voice, and very round, very gray eyes. "I believe in first impressions, Mari. And I'm always right, always. So I can tell you right now. I'm joyful for Leigh, and joyful, at last, for this house."

"Thank you," Mari whispered, touched by Phoebe's warmth.

"I believe in love," Phoebe told her. "And I know it when I see it." She paused. Then, as if reciting a lesson she had been taught long before, "I've never been in love. Never. Never. Arlene was. Once. She had a boyfriend. During the war. The First World War, that is." Phoebe turned to look at her sister. "That's why she dresses all in black. Mourning black, it is." Phoebe turned back to Mari. "I dress all in black, too, as you can see." She smiled suddenly, and licked cookie crumbs from her mouth. "It makes me look thinner," she said complacently.

Mari had the feeling, she didn't know why, that Phoebe had said, not what she was thinking, but something she was supposed to say. Mari wondered, but responded obediently to Phoebe's expectant pause. "You're not too fat."

But Phoebe was. Her cheeks were like dumplings, too round to be wrinkled. Her neck rose in round folds, like stacked doughnuts. Her body was enormous.

Again, she smiled, this time with satisfaction. But she said, "Oh, yes, I am. At least Dr. Bender says so. On the other hand, Arlene is too thin, of course. But she won't listen. Now, I want you to know, Mari. I'm the older by two years. I'm sixty-three, and Arlene is sixty-one. Sometimes she tells it the other way around, and it isn't so."

"I'll remember," Mari said, delighted with Phoebe's ingenuous sweetness.

The older woman went on, "Soon you'll be through your ordeal by family . . ." Her plump hand made a small circle. "That's the hard part, and after that . . ."

"Ordeal by family," Mari laughed, remembering that not long before she had thought she would never be able to laugh again. "That's just what Leigh called it, too."

He had been standing in front of the dressing table, staring at it with hard eyes, saying, "That's how it should be." Then, with a shrug, he had turned away. "Let's finish packing, Mari."

She had put away her things. Dresses, coat, skirts, blouses, hanging beside his suits. She carefully set her favorite book, a collection of Emily Dickinson's poems, in the top drawer of the dressing table. The book had once belonged to Mari's mother. Between its pages, Mari had pressed the yellow tulip Leigh gave to her the day they met.

She put on a dress of rose cotton, one that she knew Leigh liked, but he didn't notice that. She wore the single strand of pearls at her throat, more for luck than adornment. They, too, had once been her mother's.

Leigh had changed to light-colored slacks, a light jacket. He knotted his tie, brushed his cropped hair.

Finally, with a glance at his watch, he said, "It's nearly four-thirty, Mari. You might as well go down."

She managed to smile. "I'd feel much better, facing them with you at my side."

"I'll be along soon." He smiled. "It's only a small ordeal by family. Once done, it's

41

finished for good."

"Well, then," she drew a deep breath. "I'm off to ordeals." She looked into his face. "Leigh, I hope your grandfather can explain."

"So do I," Leigh answered.

She went into the dim hall. The green velour settee seemed to squat like an animal in the shadows. It was so quiet now that she heard the whisper of her dress on her thighs.

And then she heard another whisper, her name. "Mari, Mari, just a minute." A hoarse whisper, somehow familiar.

She stopped.

Jeff came around a corner, even bigger than she remembered him. He made a stiff, ironic bow. "I'm told that I behaved badly before. I'm told that I laughed. I'm sorry."

"That's all right." She tried to pretend that she didn't know his apology was made in sarcasm rather than sincerity. She hurried on, "I understand that you were surprised, Jeff."

"I'm also told I was rude." Jeff grinned, his small, bloodshot eyes almost disappearing into tiny pads of fat. "I say it that way because I don't really remember." His voice dropped then. He went on in a chuckling whisper. "I was drinking, you know. And when I drink . . ."

"It doesn't matter," she told him. "Truly."

"Has Leigh seen Judge Sam yet?"

"No. He's going up in a few minutes."

Jeff gave her another stiff, ironic bow. "Then I will let you go on." He stepped back, watching her without expression as she proceeded down the steps.

"Ordeal by family," Phoebe was saying. "A phrase Leigh picked up from me." For a moment, she seemed sad. Then she smiled, plainly pleased. "Yes, from me. And now, I must say a few words to Amantha. She does like her attention, you know. We mustn't offend her."

The brief warmth Mari had felt at Phoebe's words faded as the older woman waddled away, and Mari turned back to the window.

Outside, the heavy overcast broke for a moment. Bright sun painted streaks of brilliance on the tall white columns of the portico. Within, the same sun, filtered through thick lace curtains, was weakened to a misty gray. A misty gray that filled the big, wide drawing room, and all of Douglass Acres, and that seemed, to Mari, to dampen the spirits, shame laughter, and carve new lines in Leigh's face.

Yet no one, no one acknowledged it.

The circumstances which had led her to live most of her life among strangers had also taught her to read faces quickly, to study them well.

43

The Douglass women, now assembled over tea and cookies, all smiled, spoke softly, and laughed easily.

Mari saw, beyond the pretense of those smiling masks, an odd emptiness.

Below her, Jeff walked unsteadily to the big white convertible. He and Leigh exchanged a few words, then Jeff got in. Leigh nodded abruptly, and still without looking up, he spun the car around the long, curving driveway.

As it disappeared into the shadows of the arching horse chestnut trees, Mari wanted to rush after it, to cry, "Wait, wait, Leigh. Don't leave me here. Take me away with you."

Instead, mindful of the murmuring voices around her, she retreated to a big green barrel-chair.

With it protecting her back, she faced the others almost fearfully. Her small hands clenched as she waited in the refuge she had chosen, wondering why, after seeing Judge Sam for so little a time, Leigh had gone for the attorney, wondering why Jeff, too, had gone.

The pursuit, launched by Amantha Douglass, began at once.

But in those few moments while Mari was blessedly alone, she thought that it was like being lost in a room full of hungry birds.

Magpies perched on the sofa, snuggling up to an eagle. A nightingale nested on the ottoman. An aloof cardinal blocked the doorway. They were of different shapes and sizes, and wore plumage of varying hues, but to Mari they had an odd similarity. Their small puckered mouths twittered words she couldn't quite understand. Their bright eyes discreetly hooded themselves after quick, searching glances.

Mari felt as if she must be the crumb, perhaps the worm, which tempted their ravenous appetites.

Suddenly the plain gold band she wore cut into her finger. She unclenched her small fists, and dismissed her fanciful thoughts. These women were not predatory birds, but members of her family, the new family to which Leigh had brought her.

Amantha sat on the sofa, her head high, her back straight, gesturing at Mari.

Flanking her left and right were Arlene and Phoebe.

Arlene wore a scuffed Sam Browne belt that crossed her meager breasts and hung on her narrow hips. Phoebe, Mari realized, had a Phi Beta Kappa key pinned to her collar. In the doorway, Geraldine, Jeff's wife, looked like an unmoving flame in a dress of scarlet silk. Fern, now in green trousers and a matching shirt, with a braided white ribbon holding back her dark hair, sat on the ottoman, long legs angled out before her.

Mari, rising in response to Amantha's imperious gesture, told herself quickly that she was not a crumb, nor a worm, not the prey of ravenous birds. She must understand, and accept, the curiosity with which she was regarded. There was no censure in the sidelong glances, no insult in the carefully hushed voices. If anyone compared her to the woman Leigh had brought there before her, it was only natural, only right. She was, after all, thinking of that woman, too.

But she wished that Leigh had not abandoned her to the sweet, smiling inquisition which had made her hope to hide in the green barrel-chair. And as she crossed the room to Amantha's side, Mari thought that the very air of the room, the misty gray, was oppressive. Her spirits sagged even more. She was an interloper before she was known.

She sat in the space Phoebe left.

Amantha smiled. "Well, my dear. Are you all unpacked, settled in? Is there anything you need to make you more comfortable?"

"Everything is fine," Mari said.

"Good. And what do you think of Douglass Acres?"

"Why, it's beautiful, more beautiful than

I dreamed a place could be."

"We must take you on a tour one day." Amantha sighed. "If there's time." Then, "Did Leigh go up to see Judge Sam?"

Mari nodded.

"And what did he have to say?"

"I don't know. I haven't seen Leigh since."

Arlene, in a thin voice demanded, "Why does he want Henley Dunroden?"

"I'm afraid I don't know," Mari told her.

Amantha took the conversation into her own hands. "Did Leigh tell you, my dear, about Douglass Acres?" It was plainly a rhetorical question, for with a quick breath, she went on, "It is beautiful, yes. And I'm glad that you think so. But more than that, it stands for something. For a glorious and proud past, and for the present, and for a fine future too. Did you know that it was a Douglass who first built this house? This very one. As it stands. Back before the Civil War, it was. A rare family, very rare. They were Southern abolitionists, you see. They moved here from South Carolina. When this house was completed, it became a way station on the underground railroad for slaves escaping to Canada."

"I didn't know that," Mari said. She smiled, "But I ought to have guessed something. The white columns and portico . . ."

Amantha nodded. "Oh yes, the Douglass who designed it was a Southerner born and bred, and proud of it, and he left his touches here and there." Her brows rose in a perfect arch. "There are secret rooms below, in the wings, but not so secret any more, of course. And we have our legends, too. Our Old Dandy."

Mari, wanting to ask about Old Dandy, waited for Amantha to pause.

But she hurried on, sighing, "The finest place in the county, yes, even in the state . . . and to have been stricken so." She shook her perfectly coiffed white head. "The sweetest dreams die . . . the best hopes . . . strength fails . . . weakness multiplies." The words hung, fading slowly in the air. Then, "Something happened when Leigh's father died so suddenly, so awfully, so without meaning. They took Wilton out of this house, and they took its soul away. And then, Leigh went . . ."

"But he's back," Fern said.

Amantha ignored that, went on to Mari, "You're young. You're a stranger here. You wouldn't know, or care."

Mari was silent. She couldn't deny what was true. She was a stranger. She cared nothing for the red brick mansion with its portico and columns, its rolling fields. She cared nothing for its glorious past, nor its fading future. It

48

was Leigh that she loved. The Leigh she had known before she ever saw Douglass Acres, and shivered in its all-pervading gloom, and sensed the presence of an unseen, but unforgotten woman.

She was rescued by Geraldine, who drifted over to sit on the arm of the sofa beside Arlene.

Geraldine was Jeff's age, perhaps a year younger. She had a thin face marked by discontent, and narrowed blue eyes. Her hair was cut very short, shingled at the back, and a small wave lay across her forehead.

"Did Jeff speak to you?" she asked, as if none of the others could hear the question.

Mari nodded.

"Good. I told him he must. Such behavior! Honestly, I don't know what we're going to do with him."

"It doesn't matter," Mari said.

"Will you be here long?" Geraldine asked.

"Just a few days."

"Now that, my dear," Amantha said, "is something we must talk about."

"Perhaps it should be you and Leigh," Mari answered. She glanced at the window, hoping for the sound of the returning car.

"Now, my dear, between us, I will tell you that it is up to the woman of the family. It is the woman who must guide, Mari."

Mari smiled.

49

Amantha seemed to read her mind, to put her thoughts into words. "Yes, I know our Leigh. Headstrong, willful. He has always been that way, well . . . perhaps not always, but for some years now. Had he not been, he wouldn't have gone away." The small frown between Amantha's brows faded. She smiled. "But then, he wouldn't have met you."

"No, I suppose he wouldn't have," Mari agreed.

"And where *did* you meet, my dear?"

That, Mari knew, was the signal, the beginning of the sweet, smiling inquisition. She braced herself.

"It was in Amsterdam."

"In Amsterdam? A wonderful city, of course. And how did that come about?"

"I was on holiday. The spring vacation."

"And you married there?"

"No. We married in Munich."

"In Munich. Oh, yes, it was from there that Leigh wrote the wonderful news. Your parents live in Munich, perhaps?"

"I have no parents, I'm sorry to say." Conscious that all eyes were on her, that everyone was listening hard, Mari went on. "You see, I have no family at all. My mother died at my birth. That was in New York. So I am an American, of course. But in 1948, when

I was almost five, my father got a job in France. He took me with him to have me close by, I suppose. I saw him often in those days, though I was actually away at school." She paused for a long breath. "Then, when I was twelve, he died too. There was no one else. Not in this country. Not in France. He had left instructions, a trust fund to care for me. I stayed on in school, through college, until last year. Then I took a job, my first one." Mari smiled tremulously, "And that is the story of my life."

"So sad to be alone," Amantha said. "Do forgive me if I have stirred old memories. I didn't mean to pry. But I *did* want to know. And the easiest way to know is to ask, isn't it?"

"What kind of a job did you have?" Geraldine asked.

"Teaching English, and painting, too, in a small private school."

"Why, then you're an artist," Amantha cried. "How delightful."

"No, no," Mari said hastily. "I have some training, some skill, perhaps, but I'm hardly an artist."

"So you met Leigh in Amsterdam," Amantha mused. "And that was when, dear?"

"I met him at the end of April."

51

"The end of April?"

Mari smiled. "I know. I know how it sounds. You should have heard Susie — my friend and roommate, Susie — when I told her. I had known Leigh two weeks when I married. And we had three weeks in Copenhagen before . . ."

"So very romantic," Arlene said in her high voice. "That's the way it should be. That's the way it must be. When one waits . . ."

Phoebe thrust a plate of cookies at Mari. "Have one. And don't pay any attention to her. We saw a play about that. It was just the other night . . ."

"Not the other night," Arlene cried. "And not about . . ."

"Please," Amantha said sweetly. "Please, not now."

Geraldine said, "Fern, have you been up to see Judge Sam today? How is he?"

"The same as usual," Fern told her, a barely concealed sigh in her clear voice. "You know. Shaky and crabby too."

Mari caught Geraldine's sideways look.

Geraldine said, "Now with Leigh home, he'll do better, I'm sure. It will be such a comfort to him."

"Yes," Fern agreed.

"Leigh was always his favorite," Amantha mused. "Strange, strange, that it should be so. But then, Wilton was too."

"You must have more tea," Phoebe told Mari. "Come along to the table."

Mari went with her, accepted a fresh cup, refused more cookies.

Phoebe thrust a handful into her own mouth, winked. "I thought you needed rescuing." She filled another cup. "I'll just bring this to Arlene." Before turning away, she said, "You don't quite know what to make of us, do you? We're all so old, and thrown at you in a bunch. But you'll get used to the way we go on, Mari."

Left alone, Mari sat down in the green barrel-chair.

The murmuring voices went on in the background.

Fern drifted out of the room for a little while, then returned to sit near Phoebe, bending her dark head to Phoebe's white one, laughing softly at something Phoebe said. Geraldine excused herself and disappeared. Arlene and Phoebe went out, and came back with arms full of white roses, arguing about a television program.

Mari, though conscious of what was going on around her, studied the room as if it were there that she would find the answer to what lay behind those sweet smiling masks.

The rug was pale green, and soft, and richly

woven. The love seats were done in rose damask. Above the mantel a huge, gold-framed mirror gave her a glimpse of Amantha, again flanked by Phoebe and Arlene. The three women, so different from each other in appearance, were staring at her, eyes cold, mouths twisted.

Mari shrank under the impact of their looks. But then, seeing her own face, lips turned down, eyes dull, she told herself that what she had seen was a distortion, a mirage created by the imperfections of age in the old mirror.

She turned and smiled, and instantly, Amantha nodded, Arlene ducked her head, Phoebe brushed cookie crumbs from her lips and laughed.

Outside, there was a car, doors slamming.

Mari looked expectantly toward the doorway.

Geraldine, like a drifting flame, moved by.

Fern came and sat at Mari's feet, long legs bent under her. "That will be Henley Dunroden, I guess."

"I guess," Mari agreed, as Leigh passed the open doorway, with Jeff and an older man trailing him.

She wished that Leigh had paused to wave at her. She wished that he had remembered that she was there, alone, waiting for him.

"I know exactly what you're thinking," Fern said softly.

"Do you?" Mari asked. "What, then?"

"It's the most natural thing in the world for you to feel." Mari didn't answer.

"They take it all for granted," Fern said earnestly. "They don't know what it's like to be an outsider. But I do. I know. I understand."

"You belong here," Mari said.

Fern's wide gray eyes narrowed as if she had felt a sudden pain. "They brought me here when I was six. It's been my whole life. And yet . . ."

"But this has always been your home, Fern."

"I remember the other. I still remember . . ."

Mari fingered the strand of pearls at her throat.

Suddenly Fern smiled. "Did Leigh give you those?"

"No. They were my mother's."

"They're lovely." Fern's voice dropped. "I have nothing of my mother's. Nothing at all." She shrugged. "I suppose it doesn't matter."

Mari didn't answer.

"You're not a daydreamer, too?" Fern asked. "My goodness, I hope not. That's just how it started with Ellen, you know. And you mustn't be. It fuddles the wits, and drives you and drives you . . ."

"Ellen?" Mari repeated softly.

Her heart gave a small leap to hear the name, the name she had never heard before, the name of that unknown woman whose shadow lay over Leigh, over Mari herself.

"Ellen," Fern repeated. "Ellen Storer." Her voice sharpened. "Didn't you know? Didn't Leigh tell you?"

"Yes. He told me," Mari answered, knowing now why Leigh had reacted as he did at Jonah's first mention of Ian Storer, at Fern's explanation that he would be at dinner. Ellen was Leigh's first wife. Ian was related to her. But how? "Leigh told me he'd been married before."

Fern looked relieved. "Well, at least I didn't let that cat out of the bag. For a minute, I got scared. The look on your face." She grinned. "But, as I said, you mustn't be a daydreamer. Because it does fuddle the wits. You can see it does. If mine weren't fuddled, I'd never have mentioned Ellen."

"But I want to know," Mari said. "I hope you'll tell me."

Fern uncurled her long legs. She got to her feet as gracefully as a cat. "I hear the men coming down," she told Mari. "Come along and meet Henley Dunroden. It will be a rare treat for you. He's almost Judge Sam's age, and very nearly as stubborn." Her cool fingers twined through Mari's. Her voice dropped to a whisper. "We'll talk another time," she promised.

Henley Dunroden was slim, spry, dapper in a pale-blue summer suit and matching narrow tie. He had eyes like bits of chipped ice, and a dour mouth. The hand he offered Mari at their introduction was as brittle as a dried leaf. They spoke only briefly before Jeff hurried him away, yet Mari sensed that Henley had studied her and reserved judgment in that few moments.

When he and Jeff had gone, Mari made her excuses to Amantha and the others, and went upstairs, thinking that Leigh had returned to their room.

She heard Phoebe's voice raised in a querulous question, and Arlene's shrill tone replying, both of them quickly hushed by Amantha.

She felt the three pairs of eyes, as if they were actually thrusting hands on her shoulders, a pressure that stayed with her until she reached the shadows of the second floor. At the same time, pausing there for breath, she heard someone moving nearby, footsteps on bare wood, receding footsteps.

She hurried down the hall. The door to her

room was closed. She flung it open, Leigh's name on her lips.

She froze on the threshold, gasping at what she saw.

Chapter 4

The room was a shambles.

It was as if a malicious wind had scoured a swirling path from wall to wall, leaving chaos in its wake.

The tan drapes had been torn from the window and lay crumpled on the floor with the sheets and coverlet stripped from her bed. A pillow trailed snowflakes of goose-down on the brown rug. An orange lamp shade squatted in the center of the hearth. A towel hung from the fireplace mantel. Skirts and blouses, still on hangers, had been jerked from the closet and flung in every corner. An earring sparkled under the writing table. The drawers, into which she had carefully put her lingerie and stockings earlier, were crookedly open, and their contents strung around the dresser top. Its mirror, reflecting broken images, was partly obscured by jagged slashes of greasy pink.

There were murmuring voices on the stairway.

Mari drew a deep, shuddering breath, and went into the room. She closed the door gently behind her, leaned against it, too shocked to think.

But, slowly, she realized that there were small oases in the desert of destruction. Leigh's bed was untouched. The drawers of his chest were closed. There was nothing of his, nothing, in the weird litter around her.

The pattern, and the meaning behind it, was confirmed, when, drawn on unwilling feet to the mirror, she read written there in jagged slashes of lipstick the message an unknown hand had left.

MARI GO!

The crude block letters slapped at her like a crushing physical blow.

MARI GO!

Leigh. She must find Leigh. She threw herself at the door. But there, she paused, stopped once more by the sound of murmuring voices.

She must wait. She knew that she couldn't look into those sweet, smiling masks. Not now, knowing that one of them concealed wanton malice.

But which one?

Except for Amantha, who had remained like a queen on the sofa, each of them had left the drawing room at some time or other. Jeff might have been with Leigh, with Judge Sam, all the time, but also might not have been.

Who? Mari asked herself.

She backed away from the door, from the sound of those voices. She crouched in Leigh's big leather chair, the only one in the room not overturned. Who? she asked herself, staring into the fireplace. The orange lampshade squatting on the hearth seemed to mock her. She picked it up, and then went to her knees with a muffled cry. On the brushed stone, there was a scattering of faded yellow, blown like powder over tiny squares of white.

She knew, instantly, that the golden motes were all that was left of the brilliant yellow tulip Leigh had given her when they first met. The white bits were what remained of the Emily Dickinson poems, the book that had belonged to Mari's mother.

Mari touched the destroyed mementos gently, her fingers trembling. She left them on the hearth, and retreated to Leigh's chair. . . .

They had met in Amsterdam, married in Munich, honeymooned in Copenhagen. And in just about five weeks, they were back in Douglass Acres.

She knew that the facts so briefly told to Amantha had a slightly disreputable sound. That was because most of what really mattered was left out.

It was her second day in Amsterdam. She

61

had gone walking, paint box and pad under her arm, and stumbled upon the flower market beside the canal. There, in the lemon-pale sunlight of late April, with the happy shouts of the women vendors as background music, she sat down to work. Palette open on the stone wall beside her, pad braced on her knee, she began with feathery touches of green, which, to her, stood for joy and life. Joy, for the first real holiday she had ever known. For the happy cries of the flower vendors, the riotous colors, the overwhelming scent, the sun sparkling on breeze-ruffled water. Life, for the beautiful wide horizons that stretched before her. For the bright future that filled her imagination.

She was completely immersed in the odd experience of allowing her hand, detached from her mind, to do what it wanted to with brush and color. It was fascinating to see how the shadings became form, and grew substance, and spread their own patterns.

A shadow fell over the pad on her knee. She looked up, frowning, and found herself confronted by a man whose smile was so compelling, whose dark eyes were so intent, that suddenly she too was smiling. The long wordless moment that passed between them ended when he turned away.

That was her first glimpse of Leigh, and

she had seen, even then, the depths, the complexities, that later became familiar, even frightening, to her.

She watched him walk to a flower stand. He was very tall, at least two inches over six feet, and even in the bulky-knit sweater he wore, he was lithe, hard-looking. She decided that she would like to sketch him. More. She decided that she would like to know him.

She supposed that he was Dutch, though there was something about his rangy build, his stride, that seemed to mark him as different from the other men along the canal.

She smiled to herself as she returned her attention to her work. She would have an adventure to write to Susie Pryn. And Susie, being Susie, would disapprove, at the least.

But, Mari reminded herself, Susie was, after all, over thirty; and six years in the school had baked the juices of adventure out of her, so that she seemed, regardless of age, quite quite old. She was content with the room they shared, with her collection of china cups, her cats, her friends. And she wanted no more, expected no more. An exchange of smiles with a stranger in Amsterdam would strike Susie as a frivolous, if not dangerous, experience.

Mari sighed. She admitted to herself that someday she might feel the same. Dismissing that unwanted insight, she touched brush to paint once again.

And a shadow fell across her pad. She looked up.

The tall dark man had returned. Still smiling, eyes still intent, he held a clean white handkerchief in one hand, and in the other, a single perfect tulip. A tulip as brilliantly yellow as a summer sun.

While she stared at him, astonished, he touched the handkerchief to his cheek, then offered it to her.

She understood instantly, and laughed. Accepting the handkerchief, she cleaned the green paint from her cheek. She was suddenly unable to remember the Dutch for "Thank you," which she had carefully learned, along with a few other words, as preparation for her trip. So she said, *"Merci,"* hoping, since many people in Holland understood French, that he would too.

"You're welcome," he answered, his voice deep, almost gruff.

"You speak English!" she cried.

"So do you!"

"But of course I do. I'm an American." She paused then. "Well, I was born in New York anyway, and lived there until I was five."

"And you've never been back?"

"Not yet. But I will go sometime."

He sat beside her, still holding the brilliant yellow tulip. "I was positive you were a little Dutch girl. I wished you were wearing wooden shoes . . ."

They had strong coffee and tiny bitteballe at the Cafe Metropole, and later that evening, rijsttafel at the Bali. Still later, they danced in a small smoky cafe to an old-time American swing which, they delightedly agreed, was far more exciting than progressive jazz.

He asked, when he took her back to the small pension in which she was staying, "Tomorrow, Mari?"

She nodded, already sure that she ought to say she was busy the next day, and the next, and all other days that remained to her in Holland.

She, who had never known love before, somehow, miraculously, recognized it. She recognized it so well that, knowing she must not agree, she still refused to be a second Susie, she refused to be afraid. She nodded, "Yes, tomorrow, Leigh."

He looked relieved. "Early then. We mustn't waste time."

She took the yellow tulip he had bought for her up to her room, and set it in a toothbrush glass. She went to sleep dreaming of dark, somber eyes, and woke remembering them.

They had that week in Amsterdam. She, with an openness she had never known before, told him about her surrogate parents, the bank and the school, about the daydreams of her growing up.

He listened, said little. It was only lately that she realized how little he did say. At the time, she considered his reticence a product of his adulthood. A twenty-eight-year-old man did not need to prove himself by self-assertion, or by boasting. The very few men she had dated before seemed by comparison to be no more than boys masquerading in grownup clothes. She knew she would never be satisfied with them again.

She knew, too, that there was more behind his quiet, glowing smile and dark eyes than was readily apparent on the surface. She had that sensitivity developed by vulnerable people. That intuition, and the artist's eyes with which she studied him, warned her that behind his gentle manner and easy words lay a complicated temperament. She was aware of unseen currents in him, and was drawn by them. They were, surely, part of his charm.

At the week's end, Leigh put his arms around her, said gently, "I didn't know I could feel this way, Mari." He held her close, and kissed her.

But he let her go. Too soon, he let her go.

Her intuition told her that he didn't want to. Her intuition told her that he loved her. She had hoped he would ask her to stay on. But he didn't.

And the next morning, as planned long before, she went on to Munich.

She tried very hard to accept her soul-sickness. She told herself that at least she had known love once, and hadn't turned away from it. The yellow tulip, dried now, was pressed between the pages of Emily Dickinson's poems.

In Munich, Mari dutifully settled down to sightseeing. She saw little, and cared less until, one night as she dawdled unhappily over dinner, Leigh, suddenly there, said gruffly, "Mari, it was ridiculous to say goodbye."

They were married a few days later, and went immediately to Paris, where she had explanations to make, belongings to gather, a few friends to whom she must joyfully display the man who had changed her life.

Susie moaned, "But, Mari, have you gone completely mad?"

"I'm in love," she sang, dancing happily between the crouching cats.

"Yes, in love. But you don't know him. How can you? Two weeks. Just two weeks. Less even. And what will you do? Where will you live? How will you live?"

"We'll do what he wants. Where he wants to, Susie."

Mari was purposefully vague. For Leigh himself had given her few details. He had enough money for the two of them for the time being, he said. He was a lawyer, though he had never practiced. He supposed that sometime, perhaps soon, they would go back to America. He would open an office. Where didn't matter. She could choose any city she liked.

"You Americans," Susie wailed, close to tears. "Always insane, and I thought that you, with your upbringing, were different."

And Mari laughed. "You French! Always so practical, so practical, Susie, sweet. I'm in love!"

She and Leigh had three sun-filled, beautiful weeks in Copenhagen. She, intent on learning him, on understanding the complexities of his nature, found herself sometimes bewildered by his sudden withdrawals, sometimes even frightened to see his eyes turn black with shadows. But she was in love, and there were more moments, many more, when he smiled at her, smiled with a glowing warmth that made her feel like Eve, Eve, the first woman in the world, Eve, the only woman.

Three sun-filled, beautiful weeks, and then the cable arrived.

They had been at the Tivoli Gardens, wandering, with hands linked, through a magical night. A night filled with the scent of white lilacs in bloom, and with colored lanterns that gleamed like strung jewels overhead. As they left, skyrockets sent showers of exploding silver above them, and fading music trailed them along the streets.

The desk clerk called to Leigh in the hotel lobby.

She, waiting for him to join her, stared, fascinated, at the huge chandelier. It seemed to have caught the sparks from the sky outside, and now they hung above her, alive as glittering prisms.

Leigh came to her, said, not looking at her, "Let's go up."

"The chandelier is on fire," she told him. "I wish I could paint prisms. I wish I knew how."

He didn't answer. She followed him to the elevator, wondering.

Within their room, he sat heavily on the edge of the bed.

"What's wrong, Leigh?"

"It's a cable." The blue paper was crumpled in his big fist. "Sit down, Mari. I have something to tell you."

She could feel the blood suddenly drum in her ears. Her knees seemed to melt from under

69

her. She sank down beside him.

"First, the cable. It's from my brother Jeff. At home. My grandfather is ill. I'll have to go back."

"*You'll* have to go back," she said numbly. "*You'll* have to. Does that mean what it says? Are you telling me that you're going to leave me?"

"It would be best that way."

"No, Leigh. Please . . . please . . . what does it mean, really mean? Why are you leaving me?"

"It's just for a little while."

"Why can't I go with you?" She could feel herself paling. Small cold drops of perspiration formed above her lips. "Why, Leigh?"

"It would be best if you didn't. I could fly over, fly back. You can wait for me here. Even in Paris, if you like."

"Wait for you in Paris? Go back to Susie?" Mari bent her head. "Oh, how she will laugh at me."

"She won't laugh long, I promise you."

"No, Leigh. If you leave me, it will be for always. I know. I know."

"Mari . . ."

The golden highlights in her tilted eyes drowned in hot tears. Her slender body shook with controlled sobs.

He took her into his arms, held her. "Now,

70

stop it, Mari. Don't cry. Just listen to me."

She willed the tears to dry, swallowed her sobs. She buried her face in his shoulder.

"I had hoped there would be more time. A lot more time. I wanted you to trust me before . . . before . . ."

"I do, I do," she cried.

"To trust me," he said steadily, "before I told you something I ought to have told you before we were married. Ought to have, but couldn't." He sighed. "I was a widower, Mari, when we met. A man with a past, and trying to forget it." He shook his head at her small mumbled protest. "What? Does it matter so much?"

"No," she whispered. "How can it matter to me?"

But it did matter.

The questions were already forming on Mari's lips. What was her name? What did she look like? Where was she from? What did she do? How did she die? And loudest, most insistent of all, did you love her then more than you love me now?

Leigh went on harshly, "We had grown up together. Do you see? It was something that my father wanted very much. He died in an accident before I was married, but I knew that it was what he wanted. She and I had been good friends, always. And three months after

71

she became my wife . . ." His voice suddenly broke. He got up, paced the floor.

"You must have loved her very much," Mari whispered. He turned, looked at Mari, and then went on, as if she hadn't spoken. "Just three months later, she died."

"Oh, Leigh . . ."

"There was no warning, nothing. Nothing, I tell you. One day she was alive, the next dead." He returned to Mari's side. He slid an arm around her shoulders. "I left home. I left Douglass Acres. I've been traveling ever since."

"Because of what happened?"

"Only partly." He drew a long slow breath. "Mari, Mari, my love, I don't know if I can explain it even to you."

"Try," she pleaded.

"When it happened, I began to question my whole life. I, who I am, what I stand for. My family . . . everything. You see, the Douglasses are history proud, name proud. There is the fortune, maintained intact over many generations. That it still stands, as much, even more now than it stood in the beginning, is because it hasn't been dissipated, not given away, willed away, from one generation to another. Judge Sam, my grandfather, is the last of his line. When my father died, my grandfather had to make a choice of heirs. He chose me,

72

Mari. He chose me over my older brother Jeff. It wasn't discussed, of course. But I knew. I knew it in my heart. I suppose all of us did. Then, when my wife died, I didn't want to be burdened any more. I turned my back on my grandfather, on the family. I wanted to be free of them, to live my own life."

"But I don't see why, Leigh."

"No, I suppose you don't." He gave her a smile of grim amusement. "How could anybody understand without knowing that the Douglass dream requires that they all live together at the Acres. That the land, the fortune, the history never be divided? But I don't want that any more. Now, if my grandfather is ill, and needs me, I have to go. But not to stay. Do you understand that, Mari? We shan't stay there." Leigh's eyes seemed shadowed. "We couldn't stay there."

"For as long as you want to be there, at least let me be with you, Leigh," she begged. "Just don't make me alone again. I couldn't bear that, Leigh."

The next day they flew to New York.

She was awed by her brief glimpse of the city in which she was born. She hungered to see more, but within an hour they were bound for Boston, where Leigh chartered the small plane that brought them to Jessup.

And within the echoing chambers of her

anxious heart, she asked herself a dozen questions. Who was the woman that Leigh continued to remember, grieve for? What did she look like? Was she fair, dark, tall, short? Was she beautiful? Why did her presence hang like a shadow in the gray-filled rooms of Douglass Acres?

Mari, curled in the big leather chair, stirred, blinked her stinging eyes, and got to her feet.

The misty gray of the room had already darkened perceptibly.

She picked her way through the debris on the floor to the window.

Thick black clouds had flooded the sky and now hung motionless between the earth and sun, dissolving the thin gray of the earlier overcast. Thunder growled somewhere beyond the rim of the hills.

Mari couldn't bear the quality of the silence.

Her eyes went to the pink scrawl on the mirror. She turned away from it. She had to busy her idle hands, her idle mind. She bent to pick up a sketch that peeped at her from under her bed. She smoothed it carefully, then reached for a crumpled sweater.

The door opened.

Music flooded the room. Echoing shouts bounced off the empty tan walls. Yells shrilled through the broken silence.

Leigh came in. He closed the door behind him, and the invading sounds retreated. He stood there, staring at her. Finally, he whispered, "Mari, darling, what are you doing? Why have you made such a terrible mess in here?"

"What am I doing?" she cried. "I? I?" She straightened up from her crouch. She dropped the sketch, the sweater, not knowing that they fell from her numb fingers. "I? Are you out of your mind, Leigh?"

Still whispering, Leigh asked, "What are you talking about, Mari?"

"This!" she cried. "This mess, as you call it. This thing that has happened. Every small possession of mine, thrown around, every small possession destroyed. That's how I found them when I came upstairs a little while ago. That's how I found them, Leigh. And look at the mirror. Look at what it says. Somebody wrote that. Not I, Leigh! Not I!"

Very slowly, as if the movement pained him, he turned his head. He stared across the room. His mouth moved, saying silently, "No . . ."

He seemed to grow thin before her eyes. The bones in his face stood out. His eyes were dull, his mouth white.

He said hoarsely, "I shouldn't have brought you, Mari. I shouldn't have done this to you!"

Chapter 5

"No," she cried. "I know it wasn't you!"

He passed his hand over his forehead. He made an obvious effort to speak calmly. "I didn't mean that, Mari. Of course I didn't do this."

"Then who? Who?" she demanded.

The misty gray of the room turned brilliant with a lightning flash, and suddenly the walls shook and throbbed with long drumrolls of thunder.

Leigh didn't answer.

"*My* things. Just *mine*, Leigh. And you see what's written there. Mari go! Who hates me, Leigh? Why?"

"I shouldn't have brought you here," he repeated.

She remembered that she had vowed she would never make him sorry that she had accompanied him home. Yet now, within only a few hours of their arrival, he *was* sorry.

She said, "I want to know why, Leigh. I have a right to know why."

He shook his head.

"Do you want me to leave? Is that what you want? Is that why you won't explain? Tell me, Leigh."

"I'm not your jailer. If you should ever want to go . . ."

"Not my jailer!" She mocked him. "That's no answer, Leigh."

His face changed then. She saw the further effort that enabled him to grin. "I think we're becoming somewhat melodramatic over small mischief, Mari."

"Mischief!"

"Just that, and nothing more." He went to the tangled drapes, picked them up. "Look here. Nothing is destroyed. Not really, Mari. We can put everything back together again, just as it was. Nobody will ever be able to tell the difference."

She thought of the dried yellow tulip crushed into golden motes, the pages ripped to white shreds. She didn't mention those.

Silently, she began to gather her blouses and dresses, to hang them away beside his suits in the closet. She gathered her sketches, put them away.

"You see," he said in a little while. "It was just a fit of temper."

"But whose temper?"

He shrugged.

The room grew bright again with a flashing

of lightning. Thunder burst in and slowly retreated.

Mari restored the orange shade to its lamp, then turned it on.

"Did you ask your grandfather about the cable?"

"He doesn't know who sent it, Mari."

"And he really isn't ill?"

"Not that I could see."

"But then?"

Leigh hesitated. At last, he said slowly, "Never mind, Mari. In a day or two, we'll be gone. We'll leave and forget it forever."

"But why?" she demanded. "Why, Leigh?"

He dropped the gown he was holding. He took her into his arms. "Mari, no questions, please. Please," he said gently. "Not now. Just trust me, Mari."

There was a tap at the door.

Leigh's arms fell away from Mari.

She stepped back from him, suddenly cold.

"Yes," Leigh called.

The door opened. "It's me. It's your Nellie."

The woman who stood there was tiny, leaf brown. She had quick blue eyes, and a candlelight smile. "Leigh! It's made me so happy to know you're here!" she cried. "Would you believe I heard it from my brother Jonah. Not a soul of a soul in this house thought to come and tell Nellie!" She turned to Mari, "And you're the bride! Bless, you, lovey, you're prettier than my fool brother warned me."

"I should have found you myself, Nellie," Leigh said. "They said everybody was off." He grinned. "Forgive me, if you can. But since we've arrived it's been one thing after another. And I wanted to go straight up to see Judge Sam."

"Of course it's my day off," Nellie scoffed, "but when did I ever take it!" she sniffed. "You'd think the Judge would let me know. Or even Fern." She frowned suddenly. "What's been going on in this room?"

"Nothing," Leigh said quickly.

Her blue eyes made a circuit. "Again," she said softly. "Oh, Leigh, not again!"

"Nellie!"

She shook her head, "I know. I know." She bustled in, grabbed at a blouse, a dress. Meanwhile, smiling at Mari, she talked. "Lovey," she said, "your eyes are as big as saucers. I think you should begin to consider bed, a dinner on a tray, mind you. Something light, but something substantial, too. And you too, Leigh. Especially since Ian will be here tonight, hanging around Fern, he is. Courting, she calls it. I don't believe it myself. He was closer to Ellen than most brothers are to

79

their sisters, so I expect that's why he comes here." Nellie raised her head suddenly. "What are you grumbling about, Leigh?"

"Nothing," he said, his voice hard.

She shot him a bright blue look, then said to Mari, "Lovey, why don't you get into something comfortable while I do up some trays?"

"Judge Sam wants to see her, Nellie," Leigh cut in.

"Well, then, a fast visit, best for a first one anyway, I always say."

Mari, now having learned Ian's relationship to Ellen, wondered why Leigh seemed to freeze every time Ian's name was mentioned. Was it because Ian reminded Leigh too deeply of Ellen?

Nellie worked, and order appeared out of chaos. When she was through, she dusted her hands, said, "There now, all done, all forgotten." She smiled at Mari. "Did I say I'm glad to see you, lovey? Well, I am." She turned to Leigh. "Bless you for coming home, boy."

As she went out, thunder crackled again, and the window shook. Leigh closed the rehung drapes. "We should go up," he said.

Mari brushed her golden hair, first teased her bangs, then smoothed them. She powdered her nose, touched her lips with rose.

She put on tiny pearl earrings, then took them off. It was all made work, time-killing routine. She wanted a rest, a few calming moments, a chance to breathe again, before she faced Leigh's grandfather.

Leigh seemed to understand that. He waited patiently until Mari, unable to find a single thing more to do, said, "All right. I guess I'm ready."

The hallway was filled with the sounds of roaring tigers, trumpeting elephants. "Tarzan," Leigh explained. "Arlene and Phoebe really go for Tarzan."

Mari grinned.

Leigh touched her cheek. "That's better, darling. I've been waiting to see that."

They climbed thickly carpeted steps.

Once again, Mari heard sounds, sounds receding on bare wood. She asked Leigh about them.

"The servants' staircase is just behind here. It goes from the ground floor all the way up to Judge Sam's floor. He has all the rooms up here. Study, living room, business office, and a bedroom."

Leigh thrust open a door that was strangely padded with leather, and quilted with brass studs.

He led Mari into a huge room. One wall was completely glass, facing the same view that their bedroom on the floor below did. Mari recognized the yellow-gray hills in the distance.

At the end of the room, three chairs were drawn up before a fireplace. A man rose from one of them, held out his hands.

Leigh touched Mari's shoulder. "It's my grandfather, Judge Sam." He smiled, "And this, this is my Mari."

Judge Sam stood still, waiting, as Mari approached him.

He was in his middle seventies, and showed the scores and scars of time. His hands trembled, his face was deeply lined. But his dark eyes peered from under thick white brows, as bright and hard as jet. He wore a gray suit, a white shirt, and they fit loosely, as if he had not long before begun to shrink within them.

He held her hands in his, held them gently. He looked down at her, took his time, a long time, studying her, before he said in a gravelly voice, "This is a happy moment for me, Mari. You've brought Leigh home again."

"For a few days, I told you," Leigh said.

Judge Sam ignored that. "Was Jeff camping on the steps outside when you came up?"

"No," Leigh answered. "I haven't seen him since he took Henley home."

Judge Sam nodded. He gestured at the two chairs. "Sit down, children. We must talk." He lowered himself carefully into a chair that seemed, to Mari, as deep and wide as a red velvet throne.

Mari sat on the edge of a plush seat. Leigh relaxed near her.

"I'm glad that I've lived to see this day," Judge Sam said. "I'm an old man now. Old and tired, and for the first time in my life, I was beginning to be afraid. I'm afraid no longer." He paused. "If Wilton hadn't died, it would have been different. Why did Wilton die? That's the question I ask myself."

"We'll never know the answer to that," Leigh told him. Then, after a pause, he went on, "You seem very well to me."

"You deliberately mistake my meaning," Judge Sam said.

"I did?"

"Wilton would have been my mainstay. My right arm."

"I'm sure of that."

Mari, listening to the words that flowed back and forth between the two men, knew she was listening to an old argument, one that had been repeated many times.

"Now you must be my right arm, Leigh."

"I can't be. I won't," Leigh said softly.

"I told you that before I left here. I repeat it now."

"You told me." Judge Sam smiled at Mari. "But it's different now. You are different. You have reason to change your mind. The best reason, a beautiful, a sweet one."

Leigh spoke in a whisper, "More than ever I have reason not to change my mind."

"You have nothing to fear in this house. Nothing. The past is dead."

"I'm not afraid," Leigh retorted.

Judge Sam went on. "The past is dead, Leigh. Wilton gone. Ellen . . . yes, I say that name . . . Ellen is gone."

Mari glanced at Leigh.

His face was white. The shadows had bloomed in his eyes.

"They are dead." Judge Sam grinned. "Or are you as bad as the rest of them? Whispering behind my back of Old Dandy. Saying it was his candle that drew Wilton into the basement rooms, his candle that drove poor Ellen to her death?"

"You know better than that."

Judge Sam shrugged. "Do I?"

"I don't believe in ghosts."

"You don't? I realize that is the way of the young. But more fool you if you don't believe in Old Dandy." Judge Sam turned to Mari, "But he's a benevolent soul, he is. His sad

84

candles do no one harm."

"We can agree on that much," Leigh told him.

Still to Mari, Judge Sam went on. "You must explain it to Leigh. He thinks he is free. But it is not so. Not so. He is a man. A Douglass."

"So is Jeff a Douglass. And the oldest son as well," Leigh said.

"Jeff . . . now that's very amusing."

"I didn't mean to be amusing."

Judge Sam sighed, brushed a thin hand across his white hair.

Leigh asked, "Are you tired? Do you want us to go?"

"No. I would like you to join me for dinner up here. If you don't mind, that is. I'm bored with being alone."

"We'd love to," Mari said.

"And you, Leigh?"

"Of course."

"Then perhaps you'd tell Nellie?" the old man asked.

Leigh grinned, "While you work your wiles on my wife?"

"Naturally."

"I'll hurry in that case." With a small tight smile at Mari, Leigh left the room.

After an instant of silence, she asked, "Who was Old Dandy? Or what was he? I've heard him mentioned several times, but nobody explains."

"Nobody dares," Judge Sam said dryly. "I suppose that every old house must have its ghosts. A ghost is nothing more than a form of old regrets, lingering regrets, that cannot rest. The sorrow that walks because it never ends, can never end."

"And you believe . . ."

"Old Dandy was a slave. He came here, for in those days before the Civil War, this was a way station to escaped slaves. He waited for his wife. She was in her teens, I believe, and had two tiny sons. Week after week, he tended the candle in the hidden room, and prayed for their safe arrival. Finally word came that his wife had been caught, returned to her owner. One of the tiny sons had died. Old Dandy didn't believe it. He tended his candle until one night, having lost his faith, he blew the candle out, and cut his throat."

Mari's eyes went to the pewter candlesticks on the high mantel.

Judge Sam nodded. "Yes, it was one like those."

"And you believe that he still walks in Douglass Acres?" she asked in an unbelieving whisper.

"In the way I described. Yes." Judge Sam smiled faintly. "There are more things, my child, in heaven, and hell . . ."

"But my room, my clothes . . ." she stammered, picturing the malicious whirlwind that had scattered her belongings. "And why? Why?"

Judge Sam, his faint smile fading, demanded, "What do you mean?"

She explained quickly. When she saw his face change, saw how seriously he took her words, she wished that she hadn't blurted it out.

He listened silently, and when she had finished, he mumbled to himself, "Then I have been blind. Or only half-blind. Did I willfully close my eyes to what I didn't wish to see? Should I have known? Or have I always known, yet refused the truth? Am I being fair? Or am I afraid?" He sighed, raised his black jet eyes to look at Mari. "No. That's not Old Dandy's work. He sorrows. Nothing more. That is the doing of a demon."

"A demon?" Mari found herself shivering. A cold wind seemed to sweep the room. "No," she said. "No, truly, you're not trying to tell me . . ."

"I must. If I believe in Old Dandy, a ghost, then surely you can see I believe in demons too." His voice dropped. "Yes. Demons. Manifestations of evil wishes, the restless striving of unfulfilled and forbidden desires."

He paused. The brief silence throbbed with distant thunder. "Still," he went on at last, "still, you must not worry. I know how to deal with this particular demon. I promise you, you won't be troubled again."

Chapter 6

"I promise you," Judge Sam repeated, "you won't be troubled again."

Mari looked into his bright, jet-black eyes, seeking a trace of his faint smile, hoping, she admitted to herself, for an indication that within the shrunken man in his thronelike chair there lingered still a teasing youth whose solemn words were edged with silent laughter.

She sought for a trace of his smile, but she knew that he was in earnest. He had changed somehow, hardened, in those few moments it took to describe to him what had happened in the room below.

She reminded herself that he was an old man, and old men's minds are often full of confused memories and outdated ideas, and that they must be forgiven their whims. If Judge Sam wanted to believe in ghosts and demons, it was a privilege earned by his years.

She tried, thus, to dismiss his words, to seek in easy explanations an acceptable rationality. Yet she saw that he was a reasonable man and a strong one, and seemed hardly subject to brainstorms. And though she thought, "I don't believe in ghosts or demons," her hands were cold, and her heart beat slowly, slowly, an old-fashioned warning bell. She crouched in her chair, her trembling fingers twined for strength.

He, busy with his thoughts, retreated to some secret place to which she couldn't follow.

In the lengthening silence that had fallen between them, the shadow-filled room seemed to become crowded with shifting specters. Then lightning spun a quick blue light along the walls, and thunder, suddenly near again, growled a vivid punctuation to Mari's thoughts.

Judge Sam pushed himself out of his chair. "Come, Mari, I want to show you something."

He drew her with him to the wide glass wall, slid open a door, and preceded her onto a narrow stone balcony. He raised a fragile, shaking hand in a lordly gesture. "Look. Look all the way to the hills. Douglass land."

She heard the love, the pride, in his gravelly voice.

His fingers upon her arm urged her, turned her, to the view she had seen from the room just below.

Once again, she noticed the strange quality of the light. What should have been a lavender twilight was dismal gray. The yellowish hills were here and there touched by pink flickers, lightning that bloomed and faded across the valley.

"This," Judge Sam said, "this land, this house, is what I was reminding Leigh about. His responsibility. Yes, *his,* I say." The old man went on insistently. "What you can see is only a small part of our holdings. The smallest part in some ways. The rest, much larger, is perhaps more meaningful. But its value is not just in money. Its value is in my heart, too. Which is why I must know it will be maintained. Men like myself spent their lives building the Douglass fortune. Men I can understand, men I love. I do not propose to allow what they worked for to be thrown away."

He paused, but not for an answer. Rested, breath steadied, he went on. "And still, all this is only a part of my concern. I worry for Leigh. Mari, a man who lives in the past has no future. Now you will say I am contradictory, as all old men are. I speak for the Douglass tradition, and look backward over my shoulder to what is already dead. And yet I tell you that a man who refuses to let go of the past can never go ahead." His voice dropped to a whisper. "This is Leigh's responsibility. He was born to it. That is a selfish requirement on my part, I admit it. I cannot see everything built by generations be destroyed. But there is more, too. For Leigh's own sake, he must stay here. He must not run from his memories. He will be no man, no man at all, unless he conquers the fear within himself, and that can only be done here, in Douglass Acres."

"Yes," Mari said softly. "Yes, I can see that."

And it was true. For Judge Sam's words had spelled out for her the shape of her own terror. Leigh, memory-marked by the woman who had once been his wife. Leigh, remembering Ellen always. Leigh, who could never truly belong to Mari, until he laid the past away for good.

A cool damp wind lifted her bangs. She brushed at them absently.

"If you look down, you'll see the terraces, the rock gardens. I built them with my own hands, with my own hands, Mari, years ago," Judge Sam said.

She peered over the low railing. Three floors down, misted in gloomy twilight, she saw the intricate arrangement of rock and fern.

"It's not what it was," Judge Sam went on, "not any more than I am." He grinned suddenly. "I've not been down there, not there, nor in the rest of the house, since Leigh went away."

"But why?" Mari asked.

"Why? Every man has his own species of mourning."

"Because Leigh left?"

"Perhaps. Or perhaps because I do not desire the pleasure of the company of those who remain."

His face had lost years with his grin.

Mari suddenly saw what he had looked like when he was young. She recognized Leigh in the firm bones of cheek and chin, and Leigh again in the jet eyes.

"But they are your family, Judge Sam."

"Yes, indeed, and I never forget that, believe me. Poor Amantha, she will continue to concentrate on what might have been, had Wilton survived me. Poor Phoebe and Arlene, my girls with their make-believe lives. Poor Jeff, named for a great man, but weak, always weak. He has a mechanic's soul and hands, which I would respect, but he failed once and gave up forever, and now, today, he has begun to sit on the steps outside my apartment, to importune me to a decision that he knows I can never make. Fern, Geraldine, both so hopeful still. Not a true Douglass among them. Not one. I refuse to be badgered. And they have not let me alone, not since the terrible night Wilton died, and they discovered that he, like the rest of them, had nothing but that few thousand he divided between

Jeff and Leigh."

"But to live like this, alone, for so long," Mari said wonderingly.

"I'm not alone any more. Leigh is come home with you."

There were voices from within the room.

Judge Sam said, "That will be Leigh, and Nellie with him. Shall we join them?" At the threshold, he paused, raised his head. "It will rain, Mari. The storm that's been brewing all this time will break, and finally the air will clear." He went on, as if, in his own thoughts, he made a connection between his comment on the weather, and his reassuring, "Don't be afraid, child. Just don't be afraid."

As he led her into the room, a lamp flashed on. Yellow light dissolved the shadows.

Nellie scolded, "Always in the dark. I don't understand you."

Judge Sam grinned again. "You convinced me of that years ago."

"Lovey, don't mind him," Nellie told Mari. "He's just getting set in his ways." She went on, "There now. That's better. Lamplight and candlelight. Less a morgue and more a home."

Mari's gaze moved to the pewter candlesticks, now aglow with dancing flames. She shuddered. Old Dandy's lights were burning.

Nellie hurried out, and Mari turned to look at Leigh.

He smiled at her, but he said to Judge Sam, "Did I give you enough time to get your licks in?"

"I trust so," Judge Sam retorted.

"Nellie says there will be a short delay before she serves us dinner. She has apparently decided to change the menu."

"Your joining me calls for a celebration," Judge Sam said.

Leigh answered dryly, "I believe she said something about old men not eating much."

"It's her favorite theme song. I do believe that Nellie Grimes is responsible for keeping me alive."

"According to her, you haven't made it easy," Leigh told him.

"I take very good care of myself, all things considered. I've had to." Judge Sam lowered himself carefully into his big chair.

Leigh took a seat near Mari.

Nellie soon returned. She bustled around. Linen and silverware appeared magically on the table. China and fine glass came out of the cupboards. As her small brown hands darted here and there, she kept up a steady stream of conversation. "This is like a party," she told Judge Sam. "We're all together again. I have wine chilling. And steaks charring." She flicked a bright blue glance at Leigh. "And if you think I've forgotten your favorite dessert, you're wrong."

"Cherry Jubilee?" he demanded.

"What else?"

He laughed softly. "Oh, Nellie, now I'm home all right."

"You are," Nellie agreed. "So fall to." She waited, hands on her tiny hips, until the three of them had seated themselves around the table.

Then she went to what appeared to be a cupboard, and opened it. She touched a bell.

Moments later Mari heard the faint hum of an electric motor.

"My dumbwaiter," Nellie said proudly. "Judge Sam's idea. It must have saved me a million stair steps, I guess." She served the food, poured the wine.

Judge Sam lifted his glass. "To you, Mari. To you, Leigh. A long life, a happy life. At Douglass Acres."

The toast, to him, was a solemn ritual, Mari knew. She saw Leigh first hesitate, then raise his glass. She knew his reservations.

Then, with a sideways glance at her, he sipped the wine, smiled at his grandfather.

She whispered, "Thank you," both to Leigh and to Judge Sam.

"We are a family again," Nellie said, beaming at her. "This is how it is supposed to be."

But Mari, picking at her food, wondered uneasily what Judge Sam had really meant by his talk of ghosts and demons, wondered why he had told her not to be afraid.

In the glow of the yellow lamplight, she found it hard to understand the cold chill of fear which had enwrapped her before. She found it hard to understand, but impossible to forget.

"I," Nellie was saying, "recommended a tray in bed and a light supper for Mari. She's tired. She's come a long hard way since this morning, I know."

"We'll have plenty of time to recover," Judge Sam said.

"Lovey," Nellie told Mari, "don't let him browbeat you. I'll go and see about the jubilee, and check your room, and after that, you must go to bed."

"I hear a familiar tune," Leigh laughed.

"You were never one for sleep," Nellie snorted. "But time's catching up with you."

"And time enough for that, too," Judge Sam interposed. Nellie went out, but soon returned. She pressed the dumbwaiter bell, and when its soft electric hum had faded, she flung back the cupboard door, and proudly served the flaming Cherry Jubilee.

Mari, touched with sudden sadness, saw Leigh's smile, the glowing, earthy warmth that shone on his face. He looked as she had first seen him, and as she had not seem him since their arrival at Douglass Acres. She knew that he must be remembering happy moments, times before the shadows had come to darken his eyes.

She wondered if Ellen played a part in those memories too. A younger, joyful Ellen.

The yellow lamplight seemed to turn dull. The candles had burned low.

Mari heard the echo of Jeff's wild laughter, saw the crushed tulip petals. She shuddered.

There was the tap of spectral fingers at the window.

Judge Sam said, "The rain. Now the storm will break."

Leigh didn't seem to notice, but to Mari there was something portentous in the words.

She was relieved when Leigh suggested that they leave Judge Sam to rest.

"I'm not tired," the old man protested. "I feel better than I have in years."

Later on, in the midst of terror, Mari remembered his joyful look.

But then Leigh said, "Stop pressuring me."

"I? Pressuring you?" Judge Sam grinned. But, continuing, he was sober again. "Think about what I've told you. Think long and hard." He divided his dark glittering look between Leigh and Mari, so that she knew he was speaking as much to her as to Leigh. "Think," Judge Sam repeated.

Mari, full of quick love for him, would have agreed to anything then, anything to see again the grin that wiped age from his face.

But Leigh said, "I've already thought."

They left Nellie clearing up, chatting happily with the old man.

Mari breathed a noisy sigh of relief when the thick, padded door closed behind her.

Leigh took her hand. "Tired, darling."

"Just a little."

But she knew that fatigue wasn't the burden she carried. She looked up at Leigh, wondering if she could tell him about Judge Sam's ghosts and demons.

Beyond the barrier of the padded door, those frightening moments seemed more than ever unreal. She felt ashamed that some deep core of susceptibility in her had been touched, awakened.

Leigh paused at the steps, looked down at her. "What?"

"I love you," she whispered.

He was going to answer. She saw that, knew it. But a mumble of words suddenly filtered down the hallway. Shrilling music supplied a throbbing background.

He grinned. "Phoebe and Arlene are still at it." He went on.

Mari, following him, wished that he had said the words she wanted to hear. At that moment, reassurance seemed to her more important than breath itself.

A hunched shadow suddenly rose at the second landing. It swarmed up and up, spreading, wide, black. Mari jerked back against Leigh. It was as if one of Judge Sam's demons had suddenly arisen to her feet.

But Fern said brightly, "Did you have a good visit with him, Leigh?"

Leigh nodded.

"Does he know about the cable?"

"No."

"Are you really certain?" Fern grinned. "You know how he is. I was thinking . . . Leigh, do you suppose he could have sent it himself? Just to get you back?"

"He knows I'll only be here a few days. If it was a ruse, he knows now that it won't work for long."

Fern laughed softly. "You, you mustn't be angry with him, Leigh. After all, he *is* an old man. He has to use whatever weapons he can find."

"I'm not angry. But I don't think he sent the cable. It's not his style to use Jeff's name."

"But who could have then?" Fern demanded.

Leigh shrugged. "Jeff prefers to believe I

100

sent it to myself. For some nefarious reason not yet described."

"Oh . . . Jeff . . . he hardly knows where he is these days." Fern touched her braided ribbon. "What I really came up to tell you, Leigh, is that Ian's still downstairs."

Leigh's face hardened.

Fern went on quickly. "This is as good a time as any to see him." She grinned at Mari. "And to introduce you, too."

"It's late," Leigh said.

"Oh, come on now," Fern retorted. "You can't use that silly excuse more than once, and you know it."

Leigh hesitated.

Mari, watching his shadowed face, suddenly wondered if he could possibly be afraid.

"Just come down for a drink," Fern insisted. "He'll consider it peculiar if you don't, Leigh. Really, you know I'm right."

Mari, eager to meet the man who was Ellen's brother, said, "I'd like a nightcap, Leigh. It will help me sleep."

He agreed then, and went ahead.

Mari, following, with Fern beside her, saw Fern's shining gray eyes, saw the hungry look she gave Leigh, and realized with a sense of shock that Fern was in love with Leigh.

Chapter 7

Phoebe and Arlene sat together on the damask sofa, silent, side by side, like two dark shadows. They smiled vaguely at Mari, who, remembering the music in the upper hallway, the mumble of voices, realized that they had left the television alight, and wondered if she ought to mention it, but she promptly forgot her concern and the sisters when she saw the look on Leigh's face as Fern cried, luminous gray eyes aglow, "Here they are at last, Ian!"

Leigh's angular features had frozen, his dark eyes gone blank, his lips stony. He said in a low harsh voice, "Hello, Ian. It's been a long time, hasn't it?"

"Yes, a long time," Ian agreed.

He was a tall man, very thin. His hair was cut rather long, sandy, but touched with gray. His head, his face were both narrow, refined, the full lips somehow gentle, the wide-set eyes poetic.

Fern said quickly, "And this is Mari, Ian."

He turned his head, his body, turned slowly, as if he were in pain, could move only with sustained effort. His sensitive mouth curved in a questioning smile. "Hello, Mari."

Fern's laugh was husky, but unembarrassed. "I'm not very good at this, am I, Mari? Ian is our friend, and I suppose, a part of the family."

"I once was," Ian said bitterly. "But I am not any more." He gave Leigh a hard stare, and Leigh, going still beneath that look, seemed to Mari's questioning eyes to wince.

She managed to smile at Ian, to murmur an acknowledgment. But she regretted that curiosity which had led her to urge Leigh to expose himself to Ian's demanding stare.

"Isn't she a doll, Ian?" Fern cried. "So small and fair."

Once again, Mari had the strange feeling that she had become invisible. She wondered if that was Fern's intent.

Then Ian gave Mari a sudden warm smile. "Yes, you're a doll, as Fern puts it, truthfully, if not elegantly." He went on, "Welcome to Douglass Acres."

She thanked him.

But he turned back to Leigh. "So you finally came back."

Fern glowed, "Now we're all together again, the way we should be."

"Not all," Ian answered bleakly.

In the brief silence that fell, Mari sensed an unseen presence. It was as if the spirit of

Ellen had walked through the room.

Mari watched Ian as he watched Leigh. Ian's dislike was a tension-woven strand that bound everyone in its coils. They were, all of them, like players in a bad dream, moving stiffly, awaiting their cues.

Phoebe and Arlene suddenly rose. Phoebe winked at Mari. "We must see our show."

"We've missed it," Arlene said shrilly, settling her Sam Browne belt on her hips.

They went out together, arguing over whose idea it had been to stop in the drawing room after dinner.

When they had gone, Fern laughed, "Nothing changes, Ian."

"Some things do," he said, eyes on Leigh.

It was out in the open. Mari knew, understood. She needed no explanation. Ian blamed Leigh for Ellen's death. Why? Why? How could it be blamed on Leigh? And Leigh knew how Ian felt. Leigh dreaded it.

But he went to the tray on the marble table. He poured a drink for Mari, brought it to her. "You said you wanted this." He returned to make a drink for himself.

Fern joined him, leaned against his shoulder, talking softly.

Mari couldn't hear what she was saying.

It didn't matter. For Mari found herself thinking that she must have misread Fern's glowing eyes before. Fern and Leigh had grown up together, as brother and sister. It was natural that there be affection between them.

Ian sat down near Mari, his slender hands fisted on his knees, his sad, questioning eyes looking directly into her face. "You came this morning?"

She nodded. "From Paris, where we stayed overnight. But we started from Copenhagen." She added diffidently, "Our honeymoon."

"So I gathered." He gave her a quick smile, "Our Fern is a regular towncrier."

"Then you mustn't feel you have to make conversation," Mari told him.

"Why not?" His smile widened. "Is there some reason why I oughtn't to talk to you?"

She realized suddenly that he was younger than she had at first supposed. He couldn't be more than a year or two older than Leigh. But his grayed temples, his questioning eyes had fooled her.

Aloud, she said, "No reason, of course, Ian."

"You know who I am. Fern must have told you."

"You're Ellen's brother," Mari whispered.

It was a peculiar relief to say it. As if, having acknowledged Ellen's presence, Mari felt her less, rather than more, real.

"But," Mari went on, and was horrified to hear herself say it, "Don't resent me, Ian. Please don't."

"You?" His bleak gaze centered on her face. "Why should I resent you? No. No. I wish you better luck."

"What do you mean?" she demanded.

"Don't you know? Truly?"

Her heart began a quick sudden rhythm against her ribs. Her mouth was suddenly dry. She shook her head.

"He couldn't stay here. Of course he couldn't. Not after Ellen . . . died. But why not?" Ian's bleak eyes shifted to where Leigh and Fern still stood together. "And why couldn't he stay away once gone?"

To Mari, the words made sense, but at the same time, they made no sense that she was willing to accept. What was meaningful to her, meaningful in spite of her terrified rejection of understanding, was the accusation in Ian's eyes, the accusation of a guilt too awful to be imagined.

"No!" she whispered.

"But why did he come home then?"

"A cable . . ."

Ian nodded. "So I heard."

Jeff's whiskey-bloated face suddenly loomed between Ian and Mari. "If there was a cable." He chuckled. *"If!"*

106

Behind him, Geraldine put in, "But someone must have sent it."

"Perhaps," Jeff said, his bloodshot eyes on
Leigh.

Ian, with a glance at Mari, got to his feet.

"Don't let me rush you off." Jeff laughed.

Ian, ignoring him, went to get himself a
drink.

Geraldine shook her head at Mari, smiled,
and took Jeff's arm. "It's time for bed, dear
heart."

"Bed?" Jeff roared. "I'm for a refill or two
or three. We're celebrating the prodigal's return, aren't we?"

"You look as if you started before I came
back," Leigh said coldly.

"I have good cause, don't I?" Jeff chuckled.

Leigh looked down at Mari. "Ready?"

She got up. The good nights were brief.
Fern and Geraldine smiled.

Jeff boomed, "Sleep tight."

But the goodbye was one endless moment
when Ian, taking Mari's arm, asked softly,
"Why are you scared?"

Her denial was quick, emphatic, and somehow, even to her own ears, unconvincing. She
was shocked that he had read so well what
was in her heart.

Her vague apprehension, born when Leigh
told her about the cable, about his first wife,

had crystallized into fear when she walked into Douglass Acres and felt the presence there of the woman Leigh had once loved. Now, behind the family's smiling masks Mari read proof that she was an intruder, the same proof that had been so clearly expressed in the scrawl of pink lipstick that said MARI GO! on her mirror.

Yes. She was scared. Of unspoken malice. Of the unseen woman who even in death was a threat to her marriage. Of the new lines in Leigh's face.

She was afraid because she was a stranger in a house where ghosts and demons walked, and had no rest.

But she shook her head at Ian, hurried to join Leigh.

He, waiting at the door for her, couldn't possibly have heard the quick passage of words between her and Ian, and yet, as Leigh led her up the dim stairs, he said coldly, "I gather you and Ian have much in common."

"I don't know. But he seems pleasant enough."

"Pleasant enough," Leigh echoed.

In the dark upper hallway, with the dialogue from Phoebe's and Arlene's suite continuing, Mari stopped.

"Would you rather I hadn't talked to him?" she asked. Leigh, going ahead, didn't answer.

At the door to their room, he paused, took a deep, audible breath, then went in.

She followed him, prepared now for anything.

The room was golden with lamplight, and as neat as Nellie had left it earlier. There was no sign of the nightmare hand that had offered Mari its own version of welcome.

The beds were turned down invitingly. There were fresh towels on the dresser, and a huge vase of fragrant white roses.

Leigh sprawled in the big leather chair near the hearth, his face unreadable.

Mari, with a helpless glance at him, began to prepare for bed.

There was a sudden whisper at the window, a lift of the tan drapes. She stiffened, then turned slowly, carefully, to look.

"Rain," Leigh said.

"Your grandfather said there'd be a storm." She smiled. "He was right." She added, "He said after it broke, it would clear the air for good."

Leigh didn't answer.

She didn't blame him, she thought ruefully. What was there to say to such inane conversation? She went to look out.

The Douglass land of which Judge Sam was so proud was shrouded in a thick cocoon of darkness now. The hills were faintly marked ridges in a fading distance. Wind sang along the red brick walls, driving thick cold drops into her face. She closed the window, the drapes.

Leigh seemed to study with despair some private vision.

She curled on the floor, leaned against his knee.

For a moment, he didn't seem to notice, but then his hand came down, settled gently on her bright hair.

Made bold by that gesture, she said, "Leigh, it's time for us to talk."

"About what?"

"Everything."

His mouth softened with a faint grin. "Isn't that a pretty big order?"

"We could begin small," she said hopefully.

His grin disappeared. His caressing hand went still on her hair, then withdrew. He said, "If you have something to say to me, say it. If you have something to ask, ask it."

She had not yet learned to take his love for granted. She wondered if she ever would. His suddenly brutal tone seemed a complete and total rejection. Her eyes stung with quick, hot tears. She bent her head to hide them.

"Well?" he demanded.

"Leigh . . . I don't know . . . there are so many things . . . I'm confused . . . I . . ."

He cut in, "More than anything, you're tired." He added deliberately, "I think you should go to bed."

It was, and she recognized it, a final refusal. She whispered, "Leigh, are you sorry?"

"What?"

"Sorry, you brought me home with you?"

"Yes."

"But what have I done?"

He didn't answer.

"Is it because of Ellen? Does the house remind you beyond bearing? And does seeing Ian trouble you so much that . . ."

"I don't want to talk about her. Not now. Not ever," Leigh said.

"I have a right to know," Mari cried.

"If I wanted you to know, I would tell you." He was abruptly on his feet, at the door. "Go to bed, I told you."

She stared at him wide-eyed.

As he went out, she heard a thin trickle of music from the hallway. It was gone when the door closed behind him.

In the sudden silence, she became aware again of rain tapping impatient fingers at the window. She pushed herself up wearily from the rug.

The room, with Leigh gone, seemed peculiarly oppressive once more. Its austere impersonality a threat, a challenge.

She thought of her sketches, and dug them out of the closet. She studied them, each one under the golden lamplight, and finally chose two, and set them on the mantel. Two small rectangles of color. Herself in them. They spoke her defiance.

She glanced briefly at the barricaded closet, promising herself that sometime she would know what it meant. At last, exhausted, she turned off the light, lay down on the bed.

The rain whispered an accompaniment, now soft, now loud, to her frightened thoughts.

Why was there someone — demon or human, that didn't matter — who wanted to drive her away from Douglass Acres? Why did Ian look at Leigh with hatred? Why did Leigh act guilty — yes, she must face the truth no matter how it scared her — when he saw Ian? Why couldn't Leigh forget Ellen, nor hear her name?

She lay wakeful, listening for Leigh's return.

Later, when the rain stopped, she got up, opened the window, hoping for a breath of fresh sweet air. But it was still thick, damp. She returned to bed, disappointed that Judge Sam's prediction had not been right.

She dozed off, finally, and dreamed of Susie's cats, and suddenly woke with Leigh's name on her lips and the memory of a sound she had heard in sleep. And then it was no memory of a dream, but something real. An awful thudding sound that shook her, frightened her.

She sat up, peered around the dark room. Leigh had not returned.

The house was so still that she heard the faint whisper of rain dripping from the eaves.

She went to the window.

There, below her, she saw a crumpled form amid the terrace rocks, a blurred unmoving form in the shadows.

Chapter 8

For a long moment, she clung to the sill, staring into the darkness.

Then, with a panicky glance at Leigh's empty bed, she snatched up her robe, and ran.

Leigh! It must be Leigh!

She was, afterward, never able to explain why she did not cry out for help. Except that she had to get to him. She, who loved him, had to be with him. She was, afterward, never able to understand how she had managed to find her way through the unfamiliar house.

She remembered only that she spun from the window, and plunged into the breathless silence of the hallway. She flung herself down the steps, and blundered along the lower floor until, in the kitchen, she found a door that hung open on the night.

She raced into the dripping darkness, and there before her, where the terrace fell away, she saw a tiny flickering flame. A pale flame that beckoned her on. She advanced quickly, her eyes wide, staring. The pinpoint of flame became a burning candle. It had not been there when she looked down from the window. She knew that someone must be nearby. Someone had left Old Dandy's candle burning. Yet she couldn't stop. She went on, whispering, "Leigh! Leigh!"

Dark eyes stared blankly at the sky. White hair, stained black with blood, lifted on a wet wind.

Judge Sam's fragile body lay wrenched and broken, all pride abandoned, on the rocks he had once set with his own bands.

Mari threw herself down beside him. "What happened? Tell me what happened?"

Candle points danced in the dark empty eyes. White hair blew on a withered cheek.

Somewhere on a terrace below a rolling pebble sent tiny sounds into the night.

Mari leaped up. She screamed wildly, and screamed again, and turned to flee.

She managed one step, two, from the broken horror that lay beside Old Dandy's candle. Then strong arms seized her, held her. For a long still moment, she fought mindlessly.

The house was ablaze with light.

The silence became sound, raucous with shrill questions.

Phoebe sobbed.

Mari was suddenly aware, but aware only of Leigh's deep whisper, "Mari, please, don't be afraid."

She collapsed against his chest, weeping. "I

thought it was you lying there. I looked down, and thought it was you!"

"Please, Mari . . ."

"And he won't answer me, Leigh!"

Leigh set her gently aside. He bent over the fragile old man.

The others milled around in quick flutters of useless movement.

But Leigh, finally straightening up, looked at Mari, only at Mari. "I'm afraid that my grandfather is dead."

The pale gray mists swirled through the big room, smudging fuzzy outlines on whatever there was that could have been solid, comforting. Blurring the familiar faces, muting the familiar voices.

Mari didn't know if the shielding veil through which she peered was an effect of the sedative, or if, in fact, there was no veil, and what she saw was frightening reality.

She sat where Fern had put her, in the love seat. She couldn't speak. Perhaps that was the sedative too. Someone, she didn't remember who, it might have been Leigh, or Amantha, any of them, had said insistently that she was in shock, must be given something to calm her.

She couldn't speak, but she remembered exactly how it happened. Leigh looked up at her, said, "My grandfather's dead."

Amantha, white hair in wild disarray went down on her knees, moaned, "Ah, no, no. Just like with Wilton." And then, with a defiant glance directed around the circle, she snuffed out Old Dandy's candle. "There's been enough talk," she murmured, rising with the pewter holder in her hand. Now it stood on the mantel where she had put it.

Leigh carried Judge Sam's body inside.

Jeff, weeping, called Henley Dunroden.

Phoebe and Arlene clung to each other like frightened children, Arlene's thin face a wedge of pain, Phoebe's fat cheeks suddenly wrinkled.

Nellie patted Judge Sam, covered him with a sheet, cried over him.

Amantha disappeared, returned with her hair combed into its perfect chignon.

Fern leaned, swollen-eyed, against the wall.

Geraldine stared blankly at Jeff, who mumbled, "I'll never be able to show him now, will I?"

And Leigh, silent, hard as the terrace rocks, stood behind Mari, a big hand on her shoulder. He was protecting her, standing guard, she told herself. But she wondered where he had been when Judge Sam died, wondered where Leigh had been when someone lit the candle near the old man's head.

117

She looked at them, waited for them to speak, to say something about how the old man had died, about why he had died.

She looked at them, and asked herself if the demon against whom he had so earnestly promised to protect her was watching her, planning some means of driving her away from Leigh, from Douglass Acres.

She sensed the peculiar suspicion with which all of them watched her. She knew that they were wondering what she would say.

At last, she cried, "But what happened? Why did Judge Sam fall?"

Two, three voices came at once. Amantha's gentle tone overrode the others. "It must have been a dizzy spell," she said. "You didn't know, of course, Mari, but Judge Sam has had them for months. We've all worried about them, haven't we?" Her pale blue glance touched Phoebe and Arlene, both of whom nodded emphatically.

Mari appealed to Leigh. "But he was fine when we were with him."

"And when I was, too," Fern said. She looked at Geraldine. "What about you?"

Geraldine shrugged. "I thought he was tired. But he said he was O.K."

Nellie's blue eyes filled with tears. "A regular troop of visitors. I told him. I told him enough was enough. But no, he wants to see this one, that one."

"So he was tired," Amantha said, "and wanted a bit of air, perhaps wanted to look at the storm. He must have gotten dizzy while on the balcony, and stumbled, and with the railing so low . . ."

He said, Mari thought, that he felt better than he had felt in years. He said it because Leigh was home, and, yes, because he liked her, and wanted her to know it.

She whimpered, and Leigh's hand, still resting on her shoulder, tightened. His fingers became steel claws biting into her flesh.

Amantha's perfectly arched brows rose. "Mari, my dear, you're worn out. This has been a terrible experience for you."

And when Henley came with Dr. Bender, someone, it could have been any of them, said, "The poor child is in shock. She needs something to quiet her, she does, doctor."

He was a small round man, not much taller than Mari herself, but easily three of her in girth. He had a fringe of sandy hair over ears extraordinarily big, and no-color eyes behind thick glasses.

He looked first at Judge Sam, a quick but careful look, and then he came to Mari.

She shook her head in refusal.

But a glass of water appeared magically in Leigh's right hand, the pills were in the fingers

119

of his left hand. He held them to her lips, said, "Mari, swallow," and, still shaking her head in refusal, she obeyed.

Soon the big, gray-misted room began to shrink, the voices to blur, the shapes to swell, distorted, as if seen through rippling water.

Henley and Dr. Bender spoke quickly, made a few calls, consulted in low-voiced conversation with Leigh, and made other calls.

Drug-induced lethargy held Mari silent, but she remembered, and she waited. She waited for Leigh, for someone, to say aloud the words that filled her mind with echoing horror. Judge Sam could *not* have accidentally fallen to his death. She knew. She knew.

But no one spoke. Henley and Dr. Bender waited until Judge Sam was taken away from Douglass Acres. Then, they too departed, leaving the family alone.

Leigh's clawlike fingers eased on Mari's shoulder. "We'd better go up now," he said.

His face was gray-misted, like the room itself. His eyes were black with shadows.

She looked at the others, and once again imagined that they were predatory birds, their avid eyes peering at her hungrily.

The sofa heaved under her. The walls closed in. She whispered, in a voice she thought to be a shout, "There is an evil in this house.

Why didn't any of you tell the truth? Why didn't you say about the candle?"

Phoebe gasped, "Mari, no!"

"Please," Arlene sobbed.

Amantha answered quietly, "You are distraught, my dear."

It was Jeff, hoarse, his bloated face red, who agreed, "Yes, Yes." And to Leigh, "Why did you come home?"

"You know why," Leigh answered, white-lipped.

Nellie came and took Mari's hand, "Lovey, no, you don't understand. Old Dandy always leaves a candle for Douglass dead."

Mari jumped up and screamed, "No, don't blame a ghost! Judge Sam was murdered here tonight!"

The quick, burning silence of the room splintered under the lash of Leigh's hard voice, saying, "Mari, be still," while his hand once again became a steel claw at her shoulder.

She looked up, looked into his face for reassurance. Jeff said, "Yes, Leigh. And why did you come home?" It was, she knew, because of the cable. She had seen it herself, a crumpled piece of blue paper in Leigh's clenched fist. But she hadn't read it. She hadn't seen the words.

Her throat tightened with remembered panic. Leigh's bed had been empty before.

It was another gray day.

The storm had come and gone, but the air
had not cleared as Judge Sam predicted.

The thick warm mist spread across the cem-
etery, blanketing the Douglass plot, the huge
white stones, the living Douglasses who stood
beside them to watch while Judge Sam was
laid away to rest.

He was honored in death, as he had been
in life. Friends had come from as far away
as Boston. All of Jessup, all of the county,
had come to hear the eulogies, to shake their
heads over the death of the symbol of a past
era.

Mari, standing beside Ian, wished that the
terrible pretense were done.

The words were of love, honor, dedication.
To her, alone in her certainty, there was no
love, no honor, no dedication, when the truth
of the old man's death was denied.

Leigh stood apart from the others, apart
from Mari.

His hands were fisted behind his back. His
wide shoulders were hunched, under what
burden Mari didn't know, didn't dare to think
about.

She was glad he had gone to stand alone.
There was no longer any reassurance in being
with him, no comfort in the touch of his hand.

She looked at his bent head and her heart swelled with an ache she couldn't name. No, she told herself. No, it hadn't been Leigh on the balcony with the old man. Not Leigh who pushed him violently into the dark. Ian stirred beside her, slid a steadying hand under her arm. "It's hard for you," he said gently. "Just take it easy, Mari. It'll all be over soon."

She met his sad eyes. She wondered if he were thinking of that day, about two years before, when Ellen had been buried in the same Douglass plot.

The services ended. The crowd broke, moved in slow waves toward the long, black shiny cars lined in the driveway.

Mari, watching as the family assembled before their limousine, was suddenly caught in the stark terror of a moment's fantasy.

She saw them all, assembled once again, silent and in black, wearing their smiling masks as they grouped around her, grouped around where she lay in a satin-lined coffin.

Leigh's voice reclaimed her. "Ready, Mari?"

"See you at the house," Ian said.

She thanked him, grateful for the kindness he had shown by coming to stand with her when she was alone at the graveside.

In the car, Leigh was silent.

It seemed to Mari that he had hardly spoken

123

since the night Judge Sam had died.

There had been things to do, and Leigh had done them.

Yet she knew that he had seized those chores as an excuse to avoid her. Though she had felt alone for most of her life, she felt now more lonely than ever before. She couldn't bear it. She slipped her hand into his. His fingers tightened in response. They sat that way during the swift return to the house.

But, as they passed beneath the white portico, Leigh's hand fell away from hers. She was swept by a familiar sense of dread.

The big drawing room was crowded with people who spoke Judge Sam's name.

Mari offered to help, but Amantha said, "Thank you, my dear, but no. We shall manage quite nicely."

So Mari retreated to the sofa, alone again. She watched the others, thinking that each of them had his familiar chores. In the midst of grief, they performed as they had learned in earlier mourning days.

Jeff, sober now, mixed whiskey and soda for the men, and if he drank some himself, it didn't show too much.

Leigh carved the glazed ham.

Amantha served it on plates of thin china.

Phoebe and Arlene passed bread and butter.

Geraldine poured coffee, her thin face intent

above the silver urn.

Fern handed cups around on polished trays, with Ian helping.

Nellie, red-eyed, came and went quick as a bird.

Slowly the crowd thinned down. The hushed voices faded. The charade of mourning ended.

Ian came and sat with Mari for a few moments, then bade her goodbye, promising to return soon. With him gone, Mari felt once more alone, though Leigh was looking at her from across the room.

Fern came and sat beside Mari. "A long and dismal day."

Mari nodded, wondering what it was that Fern wanted to say, but hesitated over.

Fern sighed. "It's not a good welcome for you."

"I'm sorry about Judge Sam."

"Of course. We all are." Fern sounded shocked, her luminous gray eyes aglow with light. "But still . . ."

And were they all sorry? Mari asked herself. Aloud, she said, "If I only knew . . ."

"There's nothing to know," Fern told her insistently.

Those were the same words that Leigh used when, later, they had gone up to their room.

Nellie had placed a fresh bouquet of white

roses on the dresser. Fragrant scent filled the air.

Mari sat on the edge of the bed. "How can everyone pretend? If I only knew," she said wearily.

"There's nothing to know, Mari."

"The candle that appeared from nowhere?" She gave him an ironic look from almond-shaped eyes. "Or was that another one of those small mischievous pranks to which this house is so prone?"

Leigh's dark eyes were filled with shadows. "Call it that, and forget it."

"And forget Judge Sam too?" she demanded.

Leigh didn't look at her. Didn't answer.

Chapter 9

It was a hot, breathless Wednesday, and they gathered in the drawing room for the reading of Judge Sam's will.

Black clouds lay thick over the rolling meadows, over Douglass Acres.

Mari found it hard to believe that four days, nearly five, had passed since the old man's death.

She had wept for him. But now her tears were dry.

If she had not begged Leigh to bring her with him to Douglass Acres, the demon would have had no work to do. Judge Sam would still be alive, jet eyes looking at Leigh with love.

The old man had died for her. She must discover the truth for him.

Henley Dunroden, as slim and dapper as always, stood before the fireplace. Above him, on the mantel, the pewter candle holders gleamed with streaks of pale light.

His chipped-ice eyes moved slowly from one member of the family to another, his dour mouth turned down, his brittle hands steady on the single sheet of paper that they held.

"We are all here," Amantha said. "You might as well begin." She settled herself with a rustle of black linen in the green barrel-chair. "Yes, Henley, do begin."

He inclined his head. "It's very simple. And not what any of us can say is unexpected. I can tell you this will would hold in any court in the land. I drew it up myself, under Judge Sam's direction."

Henley, Mari thought, was a good enough actor to appear on a stage. He knew timing by instinct.

She wondered if he too were part of the conspiracy of silence. Had anyone told him of the candle that burned in the night?

Words spaced and weighty, he went on, "Leigh inherits the Douglass estate, and with it, all that it entails. There are are only two provisos. One: that he be here, in Douglass Acres, at the time of Judge Sam's death. Two: that Leigh be married, and his wife with him. Those conditions, of course, have been fulfilled."

Henley's dry voice came to a stop. Someone gasped in the silence. Someone coughed.

Mari looked sideways at Leigh, peering through the veil of her lashes.

His face was stony, the angular bones standing out. His mouth had tightened into a grim line.

He had said once that he wanted to be free of Douglass Acres. But she understood now why Judge Sam had so insistently told Leigh the past was dead. Leigh had been driven from home by the memories that haunted him, the same memories that lay like a shadow over their marriage. She wondered if, as he listened to Henley's voice, Leigh had felt Ellen's unseen presence between himself and Mari.

Jeff staggered to his feet. "I was so close," he yelled hoarsely. "The will says Leigh had to be here! The will says he had to be married! And it was only by a few hours, a few weeks!" Jeff's puffy face, pale then flushed, twisted. "It should have been me! You all know that. I'm the oldest son. I stayed on in this accursed house!"

"That is quite enough," Amantha said gently, her arched brows rising. "It is as Judge Sam wished. He made no bones about it, Jeff. After Wilton, it was Leigh. And it was Judge Sam's right to do as he thought best."

"I have rights too," Jeff retorted.

Amantha answered, "We are none of us, in ourselves, very important, Jeff. It is the family, what is best for it, that counts."

But Mari saw that Amantha was elated.

Mari looked at the others. Phoebe's round

face glowed with relief. Arlene was smiling her joy. Fern's gray eyes shone.

"But Jeff's absolutely right, and you all know it," Geraldine cried, flashing a malicious look at Mari. "It was just in time."

Mari clenched her small hands in her lap. She wished that she could stop her ears.

Henley said dryly, "I think I should first tell you why I was here last Saturday to see Judge Sam. Your grandfather sent for me, Jeff, so that I would answer a question which Leigh had posed. It seems he had refused the responsibility Judge Sam offered. I do not know why. That is not my business. Having refused it, however, Leigh proposed that the Douglass holdings be divided between himself and you, Jeff. It was the solution, Leigh maintained, to your grandfather's . . . ah . . . let us say, doubts. I was asked, as a disinterested outsider, what effect there would be on the fortune of such a division. I gave my opinion. I told Leigh it would destroy the family holdings forever." Henley paused. "There is one further thing." He went on, with an air of triumph, "This will was written exactly as it stands two days after Wilton died."

A peculiar pain trembled through Mari.

The words uttered in answer to Jeff's implied suspicions were like sparks smoldering in dry leaves, fuel to her own fears.

She heard Susie crying, "It's insane. You don't know him." Heard her own, "Susie, I'm in love, in love."

She had known Leigh only five weeks. Did she know him at all?

She was afraid to look at him now.

He had told her that he knew he had been chosen as the heir. He might have known about the will, with its provisos, written immediately after Wilton died.

He had married Ellen. And then Ellen died. He had left Douglass Acres. Why? He might have known about the will . . . and Judge Sam was old.

She had wondered why he chose her out of all the women he could have loved, women more experienced, more beautiful than she could ever be. But if he had married her, not out of love, but because it was time that he had a wife, then perhaps her very unworldliness had been in her favor.

Her heart contracted with self-loathing. Where in herself had she always before kept hidden the ugly core that was the source of such terrible thoughts?

And still, she asked herself if he had *pretended* to receive the cable calling him home, as a pretext for his return.

Had he murdered Judge Sam so that he could gain the inheritance he pretended he didn't want? Was she herself no more to him than a tiny part of some wild plot he had conceived? No more than that?

But she suddenly remembered that the will required that Leigh's wife be with him in Douglass Acres. Then why had he been so reluctant to bring her home with him?

Instantly the smoldering fires of suspicion died. The rippling pain of fear faded away. She told herself that she had built something out of nothing, doubts that were the flowers of the ugly seeds planted within her by the dark winds that blew through Douglass Acres.

Leigh was her love. Nothing, no one, could separate them.

Jeff growled, "There's nothing in the will to make Leigh stay here. He can take it all, and go away, and leave us here to rot."

"That's right," Henley agreed. "There is nothing but the moral obligation involved. And it has never before been abrogated. Never."

"It has never been like this before," Jeff said bitterly. He dropped his voice. "If it had been me, that's what I'd do."

Amantha said calmly, "Yes, Jeff, we've always known that."

So Mari understood then why the others had been relieved, as well as happy, at Leigh's return. Before, they had been afraid, knowing they couldn't go on without Leigh to sustain them. And when Leigh had insisted he wouldn't stay, they had become afraid again. It was a plausible explanation. Yet Mari felt there was more to be understood. What lay behind the conspiracy of silence about Judge Sam's death?

Jeff staggered from the room, Geraldine with him.

Henley said, "I thought it best for these facts to be known, Leigh."

And Leigh, silent until then, said, "No one has asked me yet what I intend to do."

Someone gasped again.

"Leigh!" Fern cried, her red mouth drawn into a grimace of pain.

Henley went on, "There's a great deal to be attended to. As I see it, you have no choice."

"If I refuse the inheritance, does Jeff, by default . . . ?"

Henley nodded. "The condition is provided for in a codicil." He added, "You do not, of course, have to refuse the inheritance, you are free to accept it, and . . ."

"Now, Henley, you know better than that." Leigh's voice was low, hard. "I either stay here, carry out Judge Sam's wishes, or I turn the place over to Jeff, and leave."

"There is no choice, of course," Amantha

announced coolly.

Leigh said, "I'll think about it for a few days. I'll let you know as soon as I can, Henley."

Amantha, her composure gone, cried, "Leigh, there is no choice!"

"I'm sorry, Amantha." Leigh's dark eyes sought Mari's.

She saw the torment in them. She realized, then, that he was trapped between two opposing needs within himself. The desire to carry out his grandfather's wishes, and the need to escape from his haunting memories, those memories that came alive in Douglass Acres.

She remembered Judge Sam saying that Leigh would be no man at all if he ran away from the past. It would follow him forever, haunt him no matter where he went.

She was determined to help him. The answer lay in the past, so she must learn the past.

As Henley gathered his papers, Mari decided that she must discuss it with him. But she had no moment alone with him. He took his briefcase, one as old as his practice, she was sure, and Leigh drove him into Jessup.

She, without being invited, went along.

The long white convertible hummed down the driveway under the white blossoms of the horse chestnut trees.

Leigh and Henley discussed problems of the estate, matters she couldn't understand. She didn't listen.

She looked at Leigh's angular profile, watched his lips move, wanting to kiss him.

She imagined how startled Henley, who seemed far beyond such hungers, would be if she were to raise her mouth to Leigh's.

She realized suddenly that she was smiling, and basked in the warmth of that moment, as if it were sun and she a flower.

But the warmth soon faded, and with it the smile.

For, as she looked back at the mansion on the brow of the hill, she remembered the questions she had asked herself, remembered those ugly doubts.

Danger lurked behind the white portico, the columns.

She thought of the pink scrawl on her mirror. MARI GO!

She thought of the awful sound of a fragile body breaking on the rock terrace, and the flickering light beside it of Old Dandy's candle.

It was the next morning, another dim, gray day. Mari wondered if she would ever see the sun again. She waited, troubled, for Leigh to join her at breakfast.

He had gone out the night before, as he had every night since their arrival, to walk, he said, when everyone else was in bed. She had awakened when he came in, and heard him stir restlessly for hours before he finally slept. When she got up, he was gone again.

Now Arlene sipped daintily at her coffee, and said in a sober whisper, "There's something I have to tell you, Mari."

Mari's heart gave a quick hard jolt. "What is it?"

"I don't know what Phoebe said, but it isn't the truth."

Mari thought, Perhaps this is the beginning. Perhaps Arlene and Phoebe. . . .

"I'm the older," Arlene whispered. "Never mind what Phoebe told you. I'm sixty-three, and she's sixty-one."

Mari laughed, amused, but at the same time disappointed. The two old ladies, sweet as they were, could be no help to her. She said, "Does it really matter?"

"I like to have things straight," Arlene said nervously.

"What things straight?" Phoebe demanded, waddling into the breakfast room.

She sat at the table, took two pieces of toast and made herself a jam sandwich.

136

"We were just talking," Mari said.

Phoebe's round gray eyes divided a suspicious glance between Arlene and Mari. "About what?"

Arlene gave in. "I was saying . . ." her thin voice broke. She began again. "I told Mari that you graduated from Goucher, Phi Beta Kappa, too."

Phoebe stroked the key pinned to her collar. "That's right. But it was a long time ago."

"And I," Arlene continued, "went to Wellesley."

"It didn't do either of us any good, did it?" Phoebe said, her usual good humor quite gone.

"We were away, weren't we?" Arlene retorted.

"And is that the only time you have been?" Mari asked.

Suddenly Arlene's thin face was blank, all expression wiped away.

Phoebe said slowly, "There was another time once."

Arlene interrupted. "Jeff never managed to get himself through college, Mari. He was at Harvard. But he wasn't serious. And Judge Sam didn't like that. Not when Jeff was dropped because he didn't study. Judge Sam was serious."

"Responsible," Phoebe said. "A very responsible man, my father."

"*Our* father, and I'd like you to remember it," Arlene cried.

"Our father," Phoebe repeated. "Yes, poor Jeff never could live that down. Judge Sam didn't let him. Judge Sam never let anybody forget irresponsibility."

"Leigh's like that, too," Arlene told Mari.

"Yes, Leigh's like that," Mari agreed. She paused. Then, "Arlene, Phoebe, you know, you can tell me. Why did Leigh go away? Why does he hate being back in Douglass Acres?"

Phoebe, her mouth crammed with toast, began to cough.

Arlene leaped to her feet, beat on Phoebe's plump back.

Mari waited impatiently until that small furor had subsided, then repeated her question.

Phoebe and Arlene exchanged a look that Mari couldn't read.

At last Phoebe said, "He's not unhappy. How can he be? He's home."

Arlene nodded earnestly. Mari saw their smiling masks. They were afraid, she told herself. They were afraid too.

She rose. "I'll see if Nellie has more coffee."

Phoebe nodded absently, "Yes, do, that's a dear." She turned to Arlene. "This morning is Concentration."

"No, Phoebe. It's my turn. Ann Sothern."

Mari left them in the midst of the argument.

In the kitchen, Nellie, in a scolding tone, told a young maid, "I don't know where you hear such things." She stopped as Mari came in, shrugged thin shoulders. "The things these children nowadays pick up."

Mari explained that she wanted coffee, thinking that Nellie ran the machinery of the household with such sure hands that the two maids who helped her were rarely seen.

"She'll carry it in for you," Nellie said, nodding at the young maid.

Mari went back to the breakfast room. She paused at the door, hearing the argument continued.

"But she can't know," Arlene said, whispering, but clearly audible.

"I think she must." Phoebe was insistent.

"No. If she did, she wouldn't ask that."

"But perhaps she was trying to find out . . . find out more."

Mari went in.

Phoebe said, "Arlene, you can be so stubborn. Think of it this way. If Maryann knows Alex is married, why should she ask Jonathon if he really is?"

It was, Mari told herself, the argument continuing. Or was it? Were Phoebe and Arlene merely two old ladies, sweet, a bit fey? Or were they clever, sly? Had Phoebe been quick enough to slip a few names, a new problem, into a discussion that Mari might have over-heard?

But what couldn't she know? Something about Leigh? About Ellen? Or was it about Judge Sam's death?

Phoebe said wistfully. "We need something nice to happen. I wish Fern would marry Ian."

"Yes," Arlene agreed. "Wouldn't that be nice?"

Phoebe's round gray look put the question to Mari.

Mari smiled agreement.

"You must tell her," Phoebe said. "Maybe she'll listen to you. She thinks she has forever. But no one ever has forever. Time passes by."

Chapter 10

"Do you remember the turtle races we used to have?" Fern asked Leigh.

They had come in together.

Fern's pale oval face was bright with laughter, her long dark hair bound back by a braided red ribbon. She wore a gray shirt, gray trousers, what Mari had come to think of as Fern's uniform.

"Do you remember that time we set up the race and then couldn't find any turtles at all?" she went on.

Leigh grinned. "I remember you all black with mud, and still digging around in the pond. What a determined soul you were."

"We needed those turtles, didn't we?"

Mari, listening, felt left out, forgotten. She had no part in that time of Leigh's life. She knew nothing about it. But she tried to picture that younger Leigh. A Leigh full of laughter, his face softer, his mouth joyful. A Leigh without the look of skepticism in his brow, without the depths, complexities which had seemed part of his charm when she first met him, but which now, yes, yes, she must admit it to herself, which now seemed frightening to her.

Leigh, still grinning, turned to her. "You're very quiet this morning."

She felt the swift curious warmth of his smile, said, "I wish I'd known you in those days, Leigh."

"You'd have had to be a tomboy to keep up with us," Fern told her. "We were wild, the three of us."

"Please pass the coffee, somebody," Phoebe put in, brushing toast crumbs from her lips.

"And for me, too," Arlene added.

Mari handed the pot to Fern, who handed it on, and then said, "Leigh, do you remember that time you dared me to climb the horse chestnut tree? And I did?"

His grin had faded. He nodded soberly.

"And how I got up there, and got down fine, but Ellen was mad, and said she could do it too. And then she got stuck and couldn't come down?"

Leigh rose without a word. Without a word, he left the room.

Mari started to follow him, but Phoebe shook her head.

"Let him be," Arlene said.

Mari sank back, sending quick glances from one face to another.

"You needn't have done that," Phoebe told

Fern, but gently.

"But what? What did I do now?"

"Ellen."

Fern looked contrite. "Oh. Oh, I see. I didn't mean to. It just slipped out, Phoebe. You know that, don't you?" She paused, then said in a brittle voice, "Besides, it was always the three of us together, and when I started talking about it . . ."

Phoebe pushed herself up, regretfully eyeing the toast platter, then, seeming to have decided against a fourth helping, she waddled to the door. Arlene, as always, trailed after her, murmuring, "Ann Sothern, Phoebe. Remember now. It's my turn."

When they had gone, Fern grinned. "Sweet. Both of them. But, oh, my . . ." She shrugged. "Not quite . . . still, it isn't their fault. Judge Sam was a martinet in his way. He wouldn't let them go."

Mari nodded. Yes. The two elderly women *were* sweet, and perhaps, having been too long within the walls of Douglass Acres, they had grown a bit fey.

"They've always been so good to me," Fern said. "And Phoebe, she's a repressed mother type, if I ever saw one. It's too bad she never had a chance to marry. But then . . ." Fern's voice changed. She grinned. "I suppose you think we're all half crazy. Amantha always moaning about what happened to her when Wilton died. The queen without her throne. And the ladies with their television sets. And Judge Sam, spouting ghost and demon talk." Her smile dimmed. "Even poor Leigh, rushing out when I mentioned Ellen's name."

"I understand that all right," Mari said softly.

"Do you?" Fern shrugged. "I don't, not really. Ellen lived. You can't pretend that away. But Ian's the only one who understands. Ian likes to speak of her. I guess it makes him feel better."

"Did she look like him?" Mari asked.

Fern's luminous gray eyes narrowed. "You're curious about her, aren't you? You keep wondering . . ." Fern shook her head. "No, Ian doesn't resemble Ellen at all. She was tall, very thin. In that, I guess they were alike. But she had very dark hair, almost black, you know. And she wore it long, and . . ." Fern hesitated, then went on, "and in spite of being rather frail, she was a real tomboy. I told you about that. She liked to wear pants. I used to say she'd wear them to her wedding. But she didn't. Oh, no, she had a veil and train of the finest lace, and a white satin gown made in Paris. She was a beautiful bride."

"And three months later, she was gone,"

Mari said. "It seams so . . . so cruel."

Fern didn't seem to have heard her. "Everybody was green with envy. Even me," she confessed with a rueful laugh. "You see, I was fat in those days, big, fat, clumsy. Nobody much loved me but Wimpy, and he'd never forget he was Ellen's dog first."

Mari laughed. "You? Fat? I can't believe it."

"I changed that. I'm determined, just as Leigh said."

Mari waited a moment, then asked gently, "Fern, how did Ellen die. Nobody has said, nobody . . . she was so young, I just don't see . . ."

Fern's hands were still. "It was just one of those things." She got up, lithe, swift, in trousers and shirt. She tugged at the braided ribbon around her long hair. "Excuse me, Mari. I have things to do. Since I don't really belong here, I try to make myself useful, you know."

"But you're one of the family," Mari protested. "Why do you say that?"

"A long sad story." Fern grinned suddenly. "I'll tell you some other time."

Mari, watching Fern leave the breakfast room, suddenly thought that she must much resemble Ellen. Tall, slender, dark-haired. Mari wondered if Leigh ever noticed the resemblance. She wondered if Leigh knew that Fern loved him.

Yet Leigh had loved Ellen. He must have loved her deeply to remember her with so much pain.

Mari told herself hastily, he loves me now. She wanted to see him, to touch him.

But Nellie, coming in with the young maid, to clear the breakfast dishes, told Mari that Leigh had taken one of the cars and driven in to Jessup.

"Now, lovey," Nellie said, "why don't you go out into the terrace, and paint one of your pretty pictures." She smiled. "Oh, yes, I looked at those two in your room. Indeed, I did, and I liked them. You mustn't think of sitting by yourself, and brooding on Judge Sam. He wouldn't like it, you know."

"But, Nellie . . ."

"Lovey, we must carry on." Her tiny hands stacked the cups. Her quick blue eyes evaded Mari's. "Go on. Do yourself a painting of the terrace. That's what Judge Sam wants."

Mari went up the stairs slowly, slowly walked down the long dim hall to her room.

A shrill, "But I don't love him. How can I marry him?" pursued her to her door. She supposed it was neither Concentration nor Ann Sothern. Perhaps Arlene and Phoebe had settled on some compromise.

146

She had hoped that Leigh had returned, would be waiting for her, but the room was empty. She went to the window.

The yellow-gray hills seemed wreathed in veils of smoke. Even the terraces below her, so much closer, were shrouded in a misty gray.

It was a poor light for painting, yet she couldn't bear the oppressiveness of the silent house.

She gathered her pad, palette, paints.

She kept her eyes resolutely away from the dressing table that barricaded the closet door which Leigh had said must always be closed. Yet she wondered what memory the closet held for him.

On the terrace, with the pad braced on her knees, and the palette lying beside her, she found herself picturing the April sun on the Amsterdam canal, remembering Leigh, and the white handkerchief he gave her, remembering a brilliant yellow tulip now crushed into golden motes and gone.

Tears stung her eyes. She brushed them away impatiently.

It would not help Leigh if she shed a million tears. She must think. She must find some excuse for going to see Henley.

She set herself to work, allowed her hand its joyful freedom. Quick strokes caught the angle of the courtyard, a wing of the house as well. She became fascinated by the play of shadows on the smudged rose of the old brick.

"You're lucky you have a way to occupy yourself," Geraldine said tartly.

Mari's golden head jerked up. She hadn't heard Geraldine approach.

Geraldine sat on a rock, brushed a thin hand along her short-cropped hair. "You'll need it," she went on.

"I wish I could do better."

"What for? It kills time, doesn't it?"

"But still . . ."

Geraldine cut in. "Leigh went into Jessup to see Henley. I guess to tell him it's all okay."

"I don't know."

Geraldine laughed bitterly. "Oh, come on. That's how it will be from now on. Leigh, Henley, and of course, you. Why should he refuse the fortune he came back for?"

"He came back because he thought Judge Sam needed him."

"Really?" Geraldine's narrowed blue eyes were intent. "Even you don't believe that."

"I know he didn't want to come back." Mari hesitated. Then, "I don't know why. Maybe you do."

"Ellen," Geraldine said softly. "That could be the only reason."

"But that's over with," Mari objected.

"Leigh didn't tell you, did he?"

"Tell me what?"

"How Ellen died."

Mari's heart gave a quick hard jolt against her ribs. She held her breath.

Geraldine said slowly, "I guess it was a bitter pill for him all right. Poor Ellen . . . she was . . . somehow . . . somehow a sensitive soul. A great dreamer of dreams, an imaginer beyond belief, a girl tender as silk. Though I must say it hadn't showed very much before. She was a tomboy then, all legs and running and Wimpy chasing her. But afterward . . . Why, Mari, Leigh ought to have told you. Ellen committed suicide."

The brush fell from Mari's suddenly numb hand. She didn't notice that she had dropped it. The pad slipped off her knees, paint leaving a long brown streak on her leg.

She stared into Geraldine's narrowed blue eyes, eyes that held obvious satisfaction at her response. She asked, "But why? Didn't anyone know why, Geraldine?"

"No. Unless Leigh knew. And he should have, of course. But he never said."

The few words, full of horror as they were, brought light into the shadows.

Now, at last, Mari understood Leigh's anguish. That his young bride should die was bad enough, but that she should have died by her own hand put upon Leigh an insupportable burden.

Geraldine rose, said, before she walked away, "Maybe Leigh will tell you about it sometime."

Mari felt her cheeks burn with shame.

Poor Leigh.

She had added to the burden he carried by doubting him. He had not wanted to bring her home with him because he didn't want their marriage contaminated by sad memories.

And here, where Ellen's death was a reproach to him, he could not forget her. No wonder he didn't want to return. No wonder he didn't want to stay. But there must have been in Ellen some small thing, unrecognized before, that led her to her death.

It could not have been Leigh's fault. He blamed himself unjustly, and had fled Douglass Acres hoping to forget. But Judge Sam was right. Leigh must forget it here, where it had begun.

Mari picked up her brush, cleaned it. She returned the smeared painting to her knees, and began quickly to repair it. Her hand shook, but the wing of the house, its strange shadows, its tiny slit window took shape under the brush.

Leigh had brought her with him because

she had refused to be separated from him. And Judge Sam had died.

A cold shiver rippled through her. The brush she held went still.

"Funny you should paint that," Ian said, from behind her.

She gasped, "Oh, Ian, you scared me."

"Sorry, Mari."

"Funny I should paint what?"

"The wing," he said soberly.

"But why?"

Ian shrugged. "No reason, I guess. Every room in this house has its secrets."

"Old houses are like that."

"Yes. They have secrets, and good reasons for them, too." He sat down beside her. "You prefer not to know, I imagine."

"I *want* to know," she said.

"Even if it hurt you, Mari?" His gentle brown eyes met her asking glance.

"It couldn't."

"Who benefits by Judge Sam's death? Who was freed when Ellen died."

"No," Mari cried, remembering her own doubts, doubts completely gone now. "No, Ian, you must be wrong."

"I'm frightened for you. Do you understand?"

"It can't be Leigh."

Ian sighed. "The wing you're painting now

is the place where Wilton died. They found him one night. His skull crushed. He had fallen down the rotten stairway that leads into the hidden room."

"Then it *was* an accident."

Ian shrugged.

Or was it really a shiver that moved his thin body? Mari asked herself.

He added, "Judge Sam wasn't the only one. There was a candle beside Wilton, too."

"Old Dandy's candle," she cried.

"That's what they say," Ian agreed. "But do you believe in ghosts, Mari?"

She shook her head slowly. She understood now that the pewter candle holders that had seemed to her to be the symbol of Douglass Acres were a symbol for death. It was no wonder that Leigh felt no enthusiasm for them.

There had been, she realized, an earlier conspiracy of silence. One when Wilton died. She wondered if there were a connection.

"I'll show you the place, if you want to see it," Ian offered.

She wanted to refuse, but some odd requirement within her demanded she see for herself, look at the rotten stairway, the underground room. She put aside the pad, the brush. She put aside a peculiar sense of danger. "Yes," she told Ian. "Show me where it happened."

He led her along the terrace to the north

wing. Close up, the old, smudged brick looked dark as blood. She didn't like that thought. She didn't like the dank foul air that came from the narrow slit window as she passed by it.

He eased open a sagging wooden door. More foul air rushed at them. A narrow staircase sloped down, disappeared into darkness.

"Careful. I'll go first," Ian said. "You keep a hand on my shoulder. We have to watch out for that step."

He moved ahead slowly. She, following, took a long slow breath.

"Stop now. Here it is. Can you step over it?"

She felt her way with the tip of her toe, and sought safety beyond the broken tread. "Yes, it's all right, Ian."

"A few more now." He reached bottom, turned to face her, led her the rest of the way down. "I should have brought a light. But you can see enough, I guess. The slit window helps some. It's where the terrace falls away actually."

It was dark, but some of the dark was less dense. Dampness drained along the crumbling dirt walls. Puddles had gathered on the earthen floor.

"In the old days, this was where the escaping slaves hid, waiting until it was safe to go on. Sometimes there were as many as forty of them, all at once, crowded here, because there was no place else to go. They were fed, of course, taken care of as much as possible. But it must have been a terrible ordeal just the same."

She imagined the tiny earthen room crowded with fearful men, weeping women. She imagined the start of group terror at every sound.

"And this was where Old Dandy waited, too," Ian said softly. "It was here that he waited alone, while his group went on to Canada. Here that he tended his candle, and waited for his family, here that he finally gave up, blew the candle out, got down to pray, and then cut his throat."

"Oh, no," she gasped.

"And Wilton came here one night, and died here."

But Judge Sam had said that Old Dandy's ghost was no more than sorrow that never ended.

"Wilton, Ellen, and Judge Sam," Ian went on. "I want you to know the risk you take. I want you to understand."

"Not Leigh. No!"

"I don't know. You don't know, Mari."

There was no air to breathe, no light to see by, no safety anywhere in the world.

154

She felt the earthen floor crumbling beneath her, and swayed. Only Ian, offering his arms, kept her from falling. She clung to him.

But faintly, through a haze of dizziness, she wondered how Ian knew there had been a candle when Judge Sam died.

She raised her eyes to his. Why had Ian brought her to that terrible place? What did he mean to do? Then she saw Leigh. She saw him leaning down at the top of the rotten stairway, his face in shadow. She saw him, and tried to call to him, but he drew back. He disappeared.

Chapter 11

Ian asked, "What is it, Mari?"

She shook her head.

"You're very pale. I'd better get you outside." Still talking, his voice gentle, he led her up the broken steps. "I . . . Mari, I'm sorry. I didn't mean to . . ." He paused, but when he closed the wooden door behind them, he went on, "I *did* mean to make you think."

She took a long slow breath, no longer afraid of him, but still afraid of the implications in his words.

She asked, "Ian, who told you that there was a candle the night Judge Sam died?" She took another long slow breath. "Fern?"

He looked confused. "Why?"

"Amantha put it out. No one has mentioned it since. They pretend it never happened."

"And with Wilton too. With Ellen, as well."

"Ellen?"

"Yes." His voice was somber. "It was there. When Leigh cut her down." Ian went on, "It was Nellie that told me. Nellie, each time. She believes in Old Dandy, you see."

"And you?"

Ian gave her a bitter smile. "You know the answer to that."

She said, her voice dropping to a whisper, "And you think they have concealed three murders? You think that, and you've done nothing about it."

Again, his poetic face was touched by confusion. "I . . . Mari, I have no proof. And there are . . . other explanations . . ."

"We must find them out then," she said soberly.

He didn't answer.

Back where she had left her pad, her paints, she gathered them together.

She waited impatiently for Ian to leave. She would listen to no more of his suspicions. She must find Leigh, explain to him why she had been in the underground room with Ian, why she had been in Ian's arms.

Ian, with a hesitant smile, asked, "Mari, can we be friends still? I've said my piece. I'll say nothing else about it."

"Yes, Ian. It's all right."

Suddenly he reminded her of Susie. She watched him go into the house. Yes. He was like Susie. He had become afraid of life. He would watch, as Susie would watch, and avoid participation just as Susie would.

As Mari went indoors, she reminded herself that she must write to Susie. A few words, a note, were long overdue. Susie would be imagining . . . Mari's thoughts trailed off. Susie could not possibly imagine what was happening in Douglass Acres.

Leigh was not in the room.

Mari, not knowing where he might have gone, decided to wait for him.

She noticed that her sketch pad was almost used up. She had squeezed most of the paint tubes dry. She wondered if there was any place in Jessup where she might be able to get new supplies.

It was moments before she realized that a pewter candlestick sat in the middle of the hearth. A tiny flame danced on a thick white candle. It sat in a pile of gray ash.

She kneeled there, staring at it. She noticed then that the room was full of smoke, full of the acrid odor of burned paint.

She looked up at the mantel. The sketches she had put there were gone. She knew that she needn't look in the closet. The whole portfolio, all the paintings she had brought with her, would be gone as well.

Her trembling fingers sifted through the ash Her work. A part of herself. All destroyed.

The demon to whom Judge Sam had given no name was determined to destroy her.

Mari jumped to her feet at the sound in the doorway.

Nellie came bustling in, her arms full of fresh towels. "Sorry, lovey, I didn't mean to scare you."

"I didn't know who it was." Mari moved to stand before the fireplace.

But Nellie's quick eyes had noticed. Her face turned as gray as the ash on the hearth. The towels fell from her arms and scattered around her. "Old Dandy!"

Mari bent then, blew out the candle.

Nellie was looking at the empty mantel. "Your pictures, lovey!"

Mari nodded.

"The wickedness, the wickedness in this house," Nellie whispered. "It grows more bold with Judge Sam gone."

"Is it because of me, Nellie? What have I done?"

"You?" Nellie shook her head. "No, lovey, not you. It has been here a long, long time. It will never end." Nellie went on, "You must be careful, lovey. I beg of you, there are things you don't understand." Her voice dropped. "You must go away. Yes. That's it. Just go away from here, lovey."

Mari shook her golden head.

"You can't fight what you can't see," Nellie pleaded.

When Nellie had gone, wringing her hands, Mari told herself that the candle-lighter was flesh and blood, and no ghost, no demon.

She must learn to fight flesh and blood, for herself, for Leigh.

She was sweeping the gray ash from the hearth when Leigh came in.

"What's that, Mari?"

He was wearing a white shirt, open at the throat, tan trousers. His short-cropped dark hair was tousled.

She thought that she had never seen him so handsome as he seemed in that moment.

"What is it?" he repeated.

She ignored the question, "Ian was showing me Old Dandy's room. Why didn't you come down? You saw us there, of course."

"I didn't think I was needed," he said with grim amusement.

She made herself smile. "Leigh! Are you suffering great and awful pangs of jealousy?"

And that word echoed in her mind. Made her think of Fern and Ian. Fern obviously encouraged Ian. Yet, Mari was sure in her heart that Fern's feeling for Leigh was more than sisterly, cousinly. Did Fern hope to make Leigh jealous by having Ian court her? And what for?

Leigh grinned. "Darling, you *were* in Ian's arms."

"You're sure of that?"

"I saw."

"You're teasing me, aren't you?"

"Just a little."

"Then don't."

He said, suddenly sober, "But I didn't like you being down there."

"Ian told me about it. He thought I'd be interested."

Leigh's tone was dry. "I'm sure." He looked at the hearth then. "What did you burn?"

She wished that she had had time to clean up before he had returned, but it was too late now. He had seen the melted candle in the pewter holder, the circle of ash, the bare mantel.

"Your paintings, Mari?"

She nodded.

"I'm sorry."

"I'll do more of them. It doesn't matter, Leigh."

He sat in his big chair, his face turned away. "But it does matter." Then, "You must go away from here, Mari."

"Go without *you?*"

"For a little while, darling."

"I won't, Leigh. That's just what somebody wants, to frighten me, to drive me away, from here, from you. But I won't give in. I won't lose you, Leigh."

"I can't leave now, Mari. There's something I have to do."

"You don't understand what I mean, Leigh. I don't want you to give up Douglass Acres. You belong here, you must stay. But I'll stay here too. I know it will be all right. We'll make it all right."

"Brave, brave words, Mari." His voice was suddenly harsh.

She wondered if he were thinking of those suspicions that he must have been able to read in her eyes the day before, when Judge Sam's will had been read.

"I'm touched by your faith," he told her, and got to his feet.

Leigh must remain in Douglass Acres, and she with him, Mari repeated to herself later.

But it was a relief to leave the somber house.

Lunch had been a dismal affair.

Jeff was even more drunk than usual, and Geraldine looked grim. Amantha, putting in her first appearance of the day, seemed to think she was entertaining recalcitrant guests, and Fern shared her pretense with her. Phoebe and Arlene behaved like chastened children, not speaking, eating quickly, and asking to be excused the moment they were done. Leigh's thoughts had plainly been far away.

Afterward, Mari, using as an excuse that she needed more painting materials, told him that she would like to go into Jessup.

He suggested, and she was glad of it, that she call Jonah. He himself, Leigh said, had work that must be done on Judge Sam's papers.

Now, sitting beside Jonah, she watched the narrow road unreel, noticing again the strange unhealthy cast of the yellowish light in the valley.

"You don't have much sun, Jonah."

"Too right," he agreed. He gave her a sideways look from beneath his peaked cap. "I hear you've seen Old Dandy, and more than once."

"Not exactly."

"His candle, then." Jonah's wizened face was serious. "Nellie told me. I know all about it. She likes you, my Nellie does."

"And I like her."

"She's scared for you."

"She won't say why, Jonah."

"Maybe there's no saying why."

"There's an explanation."

"Accidents can happen that aren't accidents. And suicides don't have to be suicides either."

Wilton and Judge Sam . . . and Ellen . . .

She accepted the implication, knowing that it echoed her own suspicions. She put it into words. "You believe they were all three murdered."

163

He plucked at his red-checked vest, and nodded.

"Why, Jonah?"

"I told you. Maybe there's no saying why."

"Who, then?"

"Old Dandy walks in Douglass Acres."

She asked, "Why do you think Wilton's death wasn't an accident?" and knew the answer before Jonah gave it.

"The candle, of course. Just like with the others."

"But someone, someone alive, put it there."

He shrugged. "Call it someone, call it Old Dandy. It's the same, isn't it?" He went on, plainly relieved, "And here's Jessup now. And it's paint you wanted. I know the place. Old Ned's general store." Jonah grinned. "Headquarters for the cab, too."

"Fine." She smiled at him, as glad as he was to change the subject. "But before we go to Old Ned's, Jonah, I want to stop for a minute at Henley Dunroden's."

"At Henley's? What for?"

Mari didn't answer.

"I guess I can find him," Jonah grumbled. "Though he's probably out to lunch, or gone fishing."

Henley, however, was in his office.

He gave Mari an unexpectedly warm smile when she asked if she could speak to him.

"Yes. Of course. Why not?" He dusted off a rickety chair, adjusted a window shade, and finally resettled himself behind his big, old-fashioned desk.

With his chipped-ice eyes regarding her, she found it hard to begin. She said finally, "I am troubled by . . . by the way things are at the house. I don't understand, and I must know."

"Yes," Henley said.

"They didn't tell you, did they?"

He raised iron-gray brows.

"About the candle the night Judge Sam died."

"The candle." Henley instead of looking surprised looked merely sad. "I see."

"Amantha took it away," Mari rushed on. "They won't explain. They won't face the fact of what it means. And what about the others? Wilton, Ellen?"

Henley interrupted, "Mari, child, you are allowing a very active imagination to find an answer to a certain set of facts. There have been such candles. Yes. Present at a particular time. Yes. But that does not mean . . ."

"But it surely means something," Mari cried.

He nodded. "Yes, surely." He paused. Then, "Have you ever considered that you have, in Douglass Acres, a rather strange sit-

165

uation. Any number of people who live there must live there, with no place else to go, no other life to live? Has it occurred to you that such circumstances can affect the . . . well, the elderly."

"Are you saying that Arlene, or Phoebe, or even Amantha, might have lit those candles?"

"I do not believe in ghosts, my child." He paused. "And I do not wish to hurt the Douglasses, any of them. Nor do you, I think. So you must put aside your foolish imaginings."

"You are convinced that Wilton and Judge Sam truly died accidentally. That Ellen committed suicide."

He nodded soberly. "Judge Sam would not thank you for bringing any scandal to Douglass Acres, Mari."

Henley, she thought, had halfway convinced her that she was mad. But as she joined Jonah, who was waiting for her, she realized that the soothing explanations did not help her.

She still did not know who had written MARI GO! on her mirror, who had burned her paintings.

"General store now," Jonah demanded.

She agreed.

The streets of Jessup were just as empty as when she had last seen them, the day of her arrival at Douglass Acres.

The big brown dog lay in the same spot in the road, and ambled away just as leisurely when Jonah blew his horn.

Jonah went into the store with her, introduced her to Old Ned, its aged owner. He beamed at her through thick glasses, and on hearing her request, went burrowing among stacks of boxes, like a squirrel in winter feed, to come up with a slightly bent sketch pad, a box of chalk, and innumerable tubes of paint. He refused payment for them, insisting, "Wedding present, that's what it is. Wedding present from me to you," and then walked away before she could thank him.

The ride back to Douglass Acres seemed too short.

Mari felt tension return to her as they rode under the arching horse chestnut trees, and parked beneath the white portico.

She lingered, talking to Jonah, until, like a reenactment of her first arrival, Jeff came down the marble steps, and stood there, wavering.

She expected him to burst into wild laughter. She waited for it.

Instead, he gave her an ironic bow. "Welcome home, Mari."

She nodded at him, paid Jonah, who whispered, "Be careful, understand me?" and drove away.

Arms laden with her purchases, she started up the steps.

Jeff said, "I thought you had maybe decided to leave."

"No, Jeff."

"It might be a good idea."

"Why?"

"Why?" He grinned. "That must be clear to you by now."

"It's up to Leigh."

"The good wife," Jeff sneered.

Mari left him leaning against a white column, chuckling softly to himself.

The pale gray mist of the house flowed to meet her when she went inside.

She saw no one, heard no voices.

She paused to admire the tapestries in the foyer, beautiful hangings, though old, time-faded. She admired the intricate work, then moved on to look at the gallery of photographs. One in particular caught her eye. It was of Phoebe, taken something like twenty-five years before. She had been plump then, but not as fat as now. Her hair had been thick, dark. She stood in front of some kind of monument, looking into the camera, her gray eyes wide, sad. There was something hauntingly familiar about the picture.

Mari, continuing upstairs, decided that she must have unconsciously noticed it before, registered it, and now seemed almost to recognize it.

The upper hallway was empty, peculiarly still. She realized that she missed the voice of the television set, and wondered why it had been turned off.

It was, she knew, nearly time for Amantha's four-thirty tea ritual. She didn't look forward to seeing again the emptiness behind the smiling masks that would greet her then.

She opened the door to her room, paused on the threshold, blinking at the shadowed darkness.

The drapes had been drawn, all light drained away. The air was thick, clammy. She knew something was wrong.

But she forced herself to go in. She had to know. She put her packages on the chair, then fumbled her way to the window.

She drew back the drapes, turned to look more carefully at the room. Yes. Something was wrong. But it took her moments to realize what it was.

The dressing-table had been moved. She saw, beyond it, the closet that Leigh had barricaded. Its door was now ajar.

She went to it, taking quick, frightened steps. She whispered through dry lips, "Who's there? Who is it?"

No one answered.

She jerked the door open. There was a faint sway of movement within. The faint sway of something heavy, something hanging. She peered, unbelieving, into the shadows.

The body of a woman hung there. Screaming, Mari turned and fled.

Chapter 12

The thick walls of the hallway seemed to muffle her terrified cry.

She tripped, and fell into the velour settee. She fought her way out of it, running again.

Mindless, as if the thing in the closet had climbed down from its knotted rope to pursue her, she fled toward the sound of voices.

It was Phoebe, plump, warm, and frightened, who stopped her. Phoebe's arms enfolded her. Phoebe crooned, "Mari, stop, what's wrong? What happened, Mari?"

Arlene's thin cold fingers caressed her arm. "What is it, Mari?"

She was drawn between the two elderly women to a doorway, and then through. Behind the three of them came Nellie, gasping, "Lovey, what's wrong?"

It was long moments before she could control her sobs, before she could look up, tell about the hanging woman.

Phoebe had turned up the volume of the television set.

Arlene had stationed herself beside the door.

Finally, gasping for breath, Mari tried to speak.

Nellie whimpered, then scurried away for spirits of ammonia, which brought Mari to choking coherence.

"In the closet. A woman. My room."

She saw that at last they understood.

Fat Phoebe and thin Arlene seemed to have turned to stone, to black, unmoving stone. The smiling masks were gone.

"A woman," Nellie repeated, shooting a quick blue glance at Phoebe, who made a small sick sound, while Arlene wept.

"Hanging there," Mari went on. "I'm sorry. I didn't mean to frighten you so. But . . . but . . . Leigh had said I mustn't use that closet, and the door was open, and . . ."

"I'll go see," Nellie said, and hurried out.

"But who?" Phoebe whispered.

"You know," Arlene answered.

"There is a madman in this house," Mari cried. "Don't you see? Don't you understand?"

The two elderly women were still as stone. "Wait," Phoebe said finally. "Wait until Nellie sees." Arlene was the first to move. She came close to Mari, taking short, jerky steps, looking as if she might fall at any moment. She patted the sofa pillow. "Lie down, Mari. Catch your breath. Lie down. Do."

172

"Yes," Phoebe said, her voice thin, faraway. "Take the afghan, and stretch out. You're all right now. It's over."

"But don't you understand?" Mari demanded, and living that terrible moment through again, she went on, "I saw the dresser moved aside, and the closet door ajar. The room was so very dark. I looked in there, and she was hanging on a rope. And she moved! I could see that she moved!"

"Don't talk about it," Arlene whimpered. "Don't think about it, Mari."

Phoebe covered her round gray eyes with her hands, moaned softly to herself.

Nellie returned, dragging something with her. She flung it at Mari's feet. "There's your hanging woman," she said.

Mari shrank back.

"Look at it, all of you. Don't be afraid. It can't hurt you. How could it? A pillow with a belt pulled around its middle. A rope of pearls where a neck might be."

Mari stared at the effigy, recognized it. She saw her mother's pearls looped at the top of the pillow, her rose-colored linen belt pulled tight around its middle.

"But why would anyone do that?" she whispered, though she knew the answer. "Why, Nellie?"

Nellie shook her head, busied her fingers

at the pearls. She untied them, gave them to Mari. "Put them on, lovey, before you lose them."

Mari didn't want to look at them, touch them, but Phoebe looped them at Mari's throat, fat fingers shaking as she linked them.

Nellie handed Phoebe the rose-colored belt. She rolled it carefully, tucked it into Mari's pocket.

Nellie fluffed the pillow, tossed it on the sofa. "All right. There's nothing left," she said.

"But who could have done it?" Mari demanded.

Nellie didn't answer.

Phoebe sighed, her round cheeks wrinkled and sagging.

Mari appealed to Arlene, who simply turned her thin face away, and once more raised the television's volume, so that the room seemed to shake with voices.

There was a knock at the door. Phoebe cleared her throat, said, "Yes?"

Fern came in. "What? A convention?" She made a face. "How can you stand all that noise?" She grinned then, "Phoebe, you'll drive us all insane."

Arlene asked innocently, "Was it too loud?"

"Oh, keep it as you want it," Fern shrugged. "I just came up to tell you that Amantha's waiting. Tea time."

Phoebe said, "I don't think I want tea this afternoon."

"Nor I," Arlene agreed.

"What? Are you both ill? Of course you do." Fern laughed. "And besides, Amantha's waiting. Ian's coming, too. He said this morning that he'd be back."

Mari slipped off the sofa. "I'll clean up first then."

"And I'll go along with you, lovey," Nellie said, taking her arm.

Mari was glad of the support. Her trembling legs felt as if they might not hold her. But she managed to smile at Arlene and at Phoebe, to say, "Thanks for the company. See you downstairs."

She made it, with Nellie's help, to her room. The closet door was closed.

The dressing-table stood before it.

"I took care of that," Nellie said. "Now you sit down and rest a bit."

But Mari could not rest. She was remembering now what she had noticed in the suite down the hall, noticed, but been unable to respond to. She was remembering how she had frightened Phoebe and Arlene.

"Nellie, I want you to tell me, right now," Mari said, "I want you to tell me how Ellen died."

Nellie closed her blue eyes, nodded. "Yes. You're right in what you're thinking. It was just that way. In that closet. And Leigh found her there, hanging, with pearls at her throat."

"And the candle."

"Yes, yes."

The brassy taste of fear was in Mari's mouth. Why was she suddenly thinking of Leigh's strong hands?

She was afraid to ask, but she had to know. "You are certain Ellen did it . . . did it herself?"

"Dr. Bender said so. Absolutely. They kept it quiet, as quiet as they could."

"How terrible for Leigh."

"Worse than any of us can know."

"Why did it happen, Nellie?"

Nellie looked confused.

"She had a reason." Mari paused. "Did she have trouble in this house? Had any of her things been destroyed?"

"There are things you don't know, lovey."

"I mean to know them. I mean to know if Ellen was driven to suicide."

Nellie's small hands twisted in anguish. "It's best if you don't. Best if you forget us all, go away from here."

"And leave Leigh?" Mari asked softly.

"If it must be that way."

"I think I can save him."

176

"Lovey, it's not something you or I can fight."

"Did Ellen have trouble in this house?" Mari asked again.

"Her dog . . . Wimpy . . . he died," Nellie whispered.

"And . . . ?"

"Her wedding dress . . . it was all ripped and torn . . ."

"Nellie!"

"Other things as well . . ."

"Messages on the mirror, Nellie? And did Leigh know?"

"He said she was doing it herself. Fern said so too." Nellie sighed. "She had lost her mind. We all knew that. But . . ."

"But what?"

"It seemed to happen so fast."

"Did Judge Sam know, Nellie?"

"We hid it from him, Mari. He was old." Nellie hesitated. "But somehow, I always wondered if he knew. He talked of Old Dandy often, of demons that walked in the night. He wouldn't go downstairs. I often wondered if he could have known."

"Ghosts and demons," Mari whispered. But she was certain that Judge Sam, using those words, meant people, people driven by sorrow that didn't end, people driven by evil desires.

She saw a connection now between what

had happened to Ellen, and what someone, a flesh and blood someone, intended for her.

To save herself, to free Leigh from his awful memories, she knew she must find the truth about Ellen, about Judge Sam.

She rose, purpose written in every movement of her slender young body.

Nellie must have sensed that. She asked, "Lovey, what are you going to do?"

"I'm going to powder my nose, Nellie, and go down and have tea with the family."

"We have so few rules in this house," Amantha said gently, her blue eyes on Phoebe and Arlene, but her words directed at Mari, "that it does seem we could manage to attempt to please one another. Tea shall be late now, and they will be disturbed in the kitchen."

Fern grinned. "I'll go back and tell them we're ready."

Amantha nodded. "Do, Fern. If Ian and Leigh are delayed, then . . ."

Phoebe mumbled, "I don't much feel like tea today, Amantha."

Mari wondered how it was possible that a few minutes could have wrought such a change in Phoebe. She seemed to have shriveled within the layer of fat that enclosed her, so that her her head bobbed on her neck. And Arlene crouched in a corner of the sofa, a frightened scarecrow.

Mari wished that she had not rushed screaming from her room. She had put the burden of her terror on the two elderly women. She must find some way, she thought, to reassure them.

She remembered suddenly that she hadn't asked them to keep silent about the effigy in her closet. She didn't want Leigh to hear of it. Yet they were obviously not going to tell Amantha, or Fern, what had happened. If they were, they would have babbled it out by now.

Amantha was saying severely, "My dears, you will soon be as uncivil as Jeff and Geraldine. But" — she shrugged regal shoulders — "if you insist, then do run along."

Phoebe and Arlene rose instantly, headed for the door like two children allowed to escape after having been kept after school.

When they were alone, Amantha smiled at Mari. "And did you have a pleasant day?"

Such social chitchat seemed ridiculous to Mari under the circumstances. She ignored Amantha's question.

She said quietly, "I found out about Ellen's death today."

Amantha's brows rose in a perfect arch. "Just today? Why, my dear, it never occurred to me that you didn't know. Leigh's marriage, poor Ellen's doing that . . ."

179

Mari burst out, "Didn't it ever occur to you that to send him to live in that room was terribly cruel?" her eyes stung with tears. "Don't you realize what it means to him, to live with such memories?"

Amantha's perfectly made-up face twisted with a grimace of distaste. "My dear, I'm afraid that you misunderstand completely. To make a great fuss about that room, about Ellen's death, is to imply that, in some way, Leigh is responsible, to assume that he must feel guilt for what is in no way his fault."

"He is troubled," Mari said.

Her doubts were completely gone, she told herself. But . . . but why had Ellen committed suicide? Why had Leigh felt that he had to leave Douglass Acres?

"Of course he is troubled," Amantha told Mari. "Whenever we lose someone we love, we must feel guilt. For after all, we believe, we must believe that love can surely conquer death, and when it does not, we feel that love has failed." Amantha paused. Then, "But to imagine, to behave for one moment, as if Leigh feels guilt, or should, at Ellen's suicide, is mad. Yes, quite mad." The sweet smiling mask slipped over Amantha's face. "All the signs were there. We didn't read them. It is impossible, don't you think, to know people really? Ellen simply lost her mind." Silken hands fluttered, "And now, let us speak of something pleasant. Wouldn't it be lovely if the sun came out?"

Amantha, Mari knew, had said just as much as she intended to say, and was glad that Fern returned at that moment.

Amantha must have shared Mari's feeling. She rose. "Perhaps you two will forgive me if I leave you to wait for Ian and Leigh?" Without waiting for an answer, she went to the door. She paused there, said, "Fern, dear, Mari has been asking about Ellen. You might explain. We don't want one of the family to believe backstairs gossip, do we?" With a final empty snaile, Amantha left the room.

"Back to her books." Fern settled on the sofa, in the place Amantha had just vacated. "That's what she does all the time. Sinks herself in books. Ever since Wilton . . ." Fern paused, "What was she talking about anyhow?"

"I offended her, I think, by suggesting that Leigh and I ought to have been given a different room."

"Oh, I see."

Nellie came in with the tea tray, poured cups full for Fern and Mari, said a few words, and hurried out.

Mari looked into Fern's luminous gray eyes, wondering how she could explain to Fern

181

what seemed, to Mari, to require no explanation at all.

"But you see," Fern said slowly. "Ellen's death had nothing to do with Leigh."

"I am as sure as you are that it had nothing to do with Leigh," Mari said stiffly, pained to realize that she, Leigh's wife needed reassurance when Fern was so certain of him.

Fern's voice was soft. "I've known him a lot longer than you have, Mari. You know the truth with your heart, don't you? As for me, I know it with my heart, and my mind, and my memory." She went on, "Ellen was a dreamer, with only half a brain, and that half concerned only with Leigh. How she wanted him, followed him around, until, when we were grown, she, being a Storer, which maybe isn't quite as good as being a Douglass, but almost as good, she won him. It was what Amantha called a suitable match. But Ellen, once she got her own way, as she always did, still wasn't satisfied. Those three months she lived here, she proved that she was mad. Wimpy died. Dogs do, you know. She claimed that he was poisoned. She ripped her wedding gown, that gorgeous one I told you about, and then tried to blame it on someone else. For heavens' sake. Who would have done such a thing? And then, the way she chose to kill herself." Fern shuddered. "You can't imagine what she looked like when Leigh cut her down. Her face bloated and black, and her tongue hanging out. Her eyes bulging over her cheekbones. It was enough to make anyone sick. I thought . . . I really thought . . . that I would die with her. Later on, I realized that she couldn't help it. We had to be sorry, to pity her. She chose the only way out."

Her choice? Mari asked herself. Or someone else's?

Had Judge Sam suspected, without having been told, what Leigh and Fern and Nellie knew?

And why had Ellen chosen to hang herself, to hang herself in the closet where she must have guessed Leigh would find her? Had she hoped to reproach him, to torment him, from the other side of the grave? Was that the reason for the lingering of her spirit in Douglass Acres?

He had said earlier, "I'm touched by your faith." Words, Mari knew, soured by bitterness, though not in the context he had spoken them.

There were rips now in the fabric of their marriage. The only way to mend them was to know the truth.

But why was Ian suspicious of Leigh?

As if she had conjured him up by thinking his name, Ian came in.

"You're late," Fern said. "Amantha has retired in a huff, and the tea is cold. And we have been sitting here," she grinned at Mari, "staring at each other."

Ian laughed. "I'll skip the tea, if you offer me a drink."

Fern jumped up, said to Mari, "Entertain him for me, will you, while I get ice and fixings?" She moved quickly, her long lithe body as graceful as a boy's in her white trousers, white shirt. "What about Leigh?" she asked.

Ian shrugged.

Fern went out.

Mari tried to imagine her fat, clumsy, sullen, but couldn't. There was nothing in her quick grace to reflect her adolescence.

"No bad effects from this morning?" Ian asked. "Old Dandy's room?"

"No." It seemed so far in the past now. The moments in the damp shadows had been lost in the closet's shadows. Mari wished that she had remembered to ask Arlene and Phoebe, and Nellie, too, not to tell Leigh about the effigy, and promised herself that in a little while, she would do that.

"But you are preoccupied," Ian said gently. "Why?"

She looked at him.

"Because of what I said?"

She ignored that. "What were they like, Ian, before it happened?"

"Fern was six when she came here. Fat, ugly as sin, and sullen. The ugliness faded fast in Douglass Acres, the sullenness, too. And Ellen was such a happy kid, until . . ."

"Until she married Leigh?"

"Yes," Ian said. "I still don't believe it. I knew her through and through. Just as I knew Leigh and Fern. They were a threesome. I didn't belong. I'm a few years older. Those years were important then. Of course, it broke up, as these things must. Leigh went away to law school. When he came back, Wilton, I never did know why, threw Leigh and Ellen together. He needed Fern, he said, for this, for that. It was obvious enough. Poor Fern, I suppose she felt left out. But she and Leigh are cousins, after all."

"Real cousins?"

Ian nodded. "Yes, though I don't know through what connections. She was orphaned, in Boston, I think. Wilton brought her here, at Judge Sam's direction, I suppose. Wilton did everything at Judge Sam's direction." Ian paused. "Except die. He did that on his own. Or . . ." Ian corrected himself heavily, ". . . maybe I should say perhaps he did."

When Fern came back with the drinks, Mari

went upstairs to see Phoebe and Arlene. She tapped at the door of their suite.

Arlene demanded, "Yes, what?" her voice muffled by the wooden panel.

"I want to talk to you two for a minute," Mari explained.

"We're napping," Arlene said. "Later on."

"It's important, Arlene."

"Not now, Mari."

"Are you both all right?" Mari asked anxiously.

"Yes, yes. We're napping."

"Later then," Mari agreed, and went to her room.

But at dinner, Nellie said, "I've taken trays up to Phoebe and Arlene. They didn't want to come down."

"Is something wrong?" Fern asked. "Shall I call Dr. Bender?"

"They say no, and I think no, as well," Nellie told her, quick blue eyes sliding a look in Mari's direction.

She, worried that she had upset them so much, stopped at their suite once more on her way to bed. But again, without opening the door, Arlene insisted that she and Phoebe were resting.

Some time during the night, a small sound woke Mari.

She sat up. "Leigh?"

"Yes."

"Are you all right?"

"Yes. I'm going for a walk. Try to sleep now."

She heard the door close softly. She slipped out of bed, went to the window.

In a few moments, she saw him move through the shadows of the terrace. He stopped, looked up.

Though she knew that he couldn't see her, she drew back. In a little while, he went on, tall, lean, dark head bent, hands in his pockets.

She watched until he disappeared into the darkness.

She thought he looked like the loneliest man in the world.

She brushed her bangs before the mirror, surprised that she saw no mark on her face of the turmoil within her.

The Friday before, she and Leigh had left Kastrup Airport, and she, looking down, had seen the green, domed roofs of Copenhagen. Now, a week later, it was another Friday.

She put her brush aside, and went downstairs.

Something, she didn't know what, made her pause beside Phoebe's picture, study the wide gray eyes, those terribly sad eyes.

Amantha asked, "You are admiring our gallery?"

Mari nodded. "This picture of Phoebe. It's a nice one."

"Phoebe never liked it." Amantha fluttered her silken white hands. "It was taken a long time ago, twenty-four, twenty-five years perhaps. When Phoebe was in Boston for a little while. She didn't even pose, you know. One of those sidewalk photographer types, in front of Bunker Hill, I think. She was too softhearted to say no to him, so she gave him the address. And it came here. Judge Sam put it up himself."

Phoebe and Arlene were in the breakfast room, two shrunken shadows in black.

Mari's heart contracted with pity for them.

But Phoebe's round gray eye winked at her. "There you are. Good morning, Mari."

"We've been looking at your photograph," Amantha said.

Phoebe examined the toast she was holding. She appeared not to like what she saw. She put it on her plate. "Have you?"

"Concentration today," Arlene said.

"Ann Sothern," Phoebe retorted.

She must, Mari told herself, speak to them as soon as she could find them alone.

She had just finished her coffee when Leigh came in.

188

He looked drawn, tired.

Nellie served him.

He ate quickly, silently. Then, for the first time since he joined them, he looked directly at Mari. "I have to talk to you," he said.

Chapter 13

There was a veil of white on the dresser top, a scattering of petals from the vase of white roses.

Mari, leaning over it, to brush the petals away, saw the pink scrawl. MARI GO! MARI GO!

She bit back the cry that rose to her lips. She made herself turn casually away, hoping that Leigh hadn't noticed.

He was at the window, bracing himself with fists at the sill. He said, not looking at her, "I've moved my things out of here, Mari. I'll be staying in Judge Sam's apartment for a while."

It was a measure of how deeply she was infected by the contagion in the house that she didn't immediately protest.

First she asked herself what he was thinking behind the brooding look in his eyes. Then she asked herself what his sudden need for privacy meant.

Finally, aloud, she demanded, "But why, Leigh?"

"I disturb you," he said tonelessly. "I know that you hear me go out to walk every night.

I know I woke you last night, and the night before that."

"It doesn't matter, Leigh."

"You need your rest, Mari."

She shook her head, brushed at her golden bangs. "Oh, Leigh, what have I done?"

"You? Nothing."

So she knew Judge Sam's demon had scored again.

Leigh had, in the days since the funeral, tended to avoid her. He spent most of his time walking on the terraces, the rest of it working in the third-floor apartment, or in town with Henley.

This was one more move to make concrete the withdrawal from her which she had sensed since they came to Douglass Acres.

She said gently, "Leigh, listen, I realize that this room is terrible for you. After what happened here, you . . ."

"I don't want to talk about that, Mari."

"Is it me that you can't bear? Or is it the memory of Ellen?"

"Stop it, Mari."

But she couldn't stop herself. She whispered, "Leigh, don't you know that I don't care what you've done? I love you. I don't care."

His shadowed eyes blazed with sudden fury. "And what have I done?"

191

"I don't know," she cried. "I told you, I don't care."

"You don't care," he repeated, through clenched teeth.

He wasn't the man she knew, the man she had married. When he came to her, when his hands fell heavily on her shoulders, she shrank back.

The blaze faded from his eyes. He let her go. "Mari, Mari, darling, are you afraid of *me?*" he asked hoarsely.

"Oh, Leigh, no!"

But she knew that the seeds of doubt in her had amounted to betrayal. She hated herself in that instant, for out of fear, she had failed her love. Wanting to help him, she had hurt him.

She said softly now, too late, "Leigh, believe me, nothing is changed between us."

But he was no longer listening. She saw that he stared past her shoulder, dark eyes narrowed.

He moved her gently aside, and bent over the dressing table. He brushed the veil of fallen rose petals away.

"Mari Go!" he whispered. He turned to her. "You saw it when you first came in, didn't you?"

She nodded.

"Why didn't you tell me?"

"It wasn't worth mentioning."

"Mari . . ."

"All right, Leigh. I was afraid you'd say I have to leave."

"Yes. Then we don't have to argue about it, do we?"

"I will not go, not alone, Leigh."

He hesitated. Then, "Mari, I've been forced to a decision. One I didn't think I would ever make. I can't turn my back on all the lives at stake."

"Then I will stay too!"

"No, Mari."

"Why do you want to drive me away?"

"You must know the answer to that."

"I don't know it, Leigh."

"Then you won't believe the only answer I can give you, Mari."

"I won't leave you," she said.

He gave her a look she couldn't read. He answered slowly, "I hope you're never sorry, darling."

More than ever, she was determined that he not hear about the belt-shaped pillow that had been hung in the closet.

When she thought he had left the hallway, she went to the suite in the north wing. A machinegun stuttered viciously through the doorway, a faint voice screamed, another sobbed.

Mari knocked, went in.

Phoebe and Arlene were standing at opposite ends of the room. They looked as if they had been pacing back and forth, and had frozen when she came

Phoebe looked ill, tired.

Arlene mumbled, "We're resting, Mari."

"I won't stay but a minute. I wanted to know first if you're all right? And then, I . . . well, I wanted to say I was sorry. I oughtn't to have come in here yesterday the way I did. I know I scared you terribly. But it's O.K., you know. Just forget about it, both of you. I don't want you to worry. So forget it happened. And don't . . . you won't tell Leigh, will you?"

Phoebe shook her head, her face flushed.

"Fern was asking if you needed Dr. Bender. Perhaps . . . ?"

Phoebe's placid expression suddenly broke. She let out a wail. She stumbled to the sofa and collapsed into it, like a punctured balloon. "I can't, Arlene. I can't, I can't," she moaned.

Arlene sat down beside her.

Mari was startled by the expression on the thin woman's face. She looked peculiarly unmoved, unsympathetic. As if she had witnessed Phoebe's tears too many times before to react.

But Mari, shaken, cried, "What can I do?"

"It's all right," Arlene assured her. "We'll be all right. If you leave us alone."

Mari tiptoed from the room. The machine-gun's stutter followed her.

She didn't know why, but she was drawn to the downstairs hallway, to the gallery of photographs, to the old picture of Phoebe that hung there. She decided to have one more look at it, a careful look. Perhaps she would see, finally, why it seemed familiar to her.

She went to the corner, sought Phoebe's sad eyes. The picture was gone.

She checked the whole bank of photographs, thinking she had mistaken the spot it had been in. No, the one of Phoebe was not there.

Bewildered, she asked Nellie about it.

Nellie shrugged. "I never noticed."

Mari remembered the day before. "You haven't told Leigh, have you? You won't tell him what happened?"

"He should know," Nellie said dubiously. "I just assumed that you . . ."

"I don't want him to worry. Promise me, Nellie."

Nellie agreed, still dubious, and Mari went out to the terrace. But she soon retreated indoors to escape the warm gray air. The day dragged by.

She exchanged a few words with Fern, a

few with Geraldine. Amantha remained behind the draped double doors of her rooms.

Mari was glad when at last night came. But when she went to bed, she listened to the whispers that spread through the old house.

She thought that Douglass Acres had a nighttime voice, and a daytime voice. By dark the words were full of menace, by day they were falsely sweet, gentle.

Somewhere women laughed, and men whistled, and children cried, and then slept, comforted, in their mother's arms. Somewhere there was love. But Douglass Acres drifted in a strange isolation, a world to itself within that other world.

With Leigh gone, the room seemed empty, more oppressive than ever. His big chair a crouching bear, the chest of drawers some unspeakable thing. The closet door, once more barricaded by the dressing table, was the lid to Pandora's box. Closed in actuality, but opened in memory. And containing the limp body of a hanging woman.

Why wouldn't Leigh allow Ellen's name to be said in his hearing? What did that mean? Why had he first left Douglass Acres? And why, now that he could leave once more, did he feel he must stay? Why had he left her to suffer through the fearful night alone, and moved so far away as the third-floor apartment?

The fear she had first felt in Douglass Acres seemed to have spread through her, the distrust to have soiled her every thought.

She asked herself if Jeff and Geraldine, hating Leigh, wanting themselves to inherit, were trying to drive her, and with her, Leigh, away. If Amantha, regal Amantha, wanted Leigh to herself so that she could rule Douglass Acres with him, as she might once have ruled with Wilton. If Arlene and Phoebe were as sweet, frightened, as they seem. Or if, as Henley had implied, they were controlled by a hidden madness. If they hated love, having never known it, and had to see it destroyed. If Fern . . . open and forthright Fern, who was, like Mari herself, an outsider . . .

At last exhausted in the midst of her anxious speculations, Mari fell asleep.

She dressed carefully in the gray morning light. She chose a sleeveless red cotton, because red was for cheer. She brushed her golden hair, and teased her bangs, and then brushed them smooth again. She put on her pearls, and shuddered at the image of the effigy that leaped instantly into her mind, but she was determined not to allow that memory to spoil the one thing remaining that her mother had left to her.

The pearls were her talisman. With that thought, she went in search of Leigh.

He was not in the breakfast room. She lingered over coffee, hoping that he would come down. Then Nellie said, "Lovey, Leigh's been in for coffee with Fern, and left hours ago."

The sympathy in Nellie's voice brought quick tears to Mari's eyes.

When she could talk, she asked, "Did he go upstairs?"

"Why don't you run up and see?"

So Mari knew that everyone in the house understood that the demon had scored. She hadn't left Leigh, so he had left her.

The Saturday before, she had come to Douglass Acres, fearing the shadow of an unknown woman. Now that woman was known.

And now Mari feared that the love she had believed in then was gone, perhaps had never been.

She climbed the stairs slowly, small unspoken prayers rippling through her mind. She wanted only a sign, a tiny sign, that Leigh still loved her. She didn't know what she would say to him. She trusted that when the moment came, her heart would tell her, and she would tell him. If he would give her the opportunity to.

She paused at the second-floor landing. It was dim, the television set silent. It seemed wrong somehow that the mellow voices, the wailing words, were not pouring out of Phoebe's and Arlene's suite. The third-floor hall was almost dark, as if night instead of morning dwelled there.

She paused before the padded, brass-studded door, then knocked. She waited, listening for a response. Then, when there was none, she knocked harder. Finally, with no answer forthcoming, she pushed open the heavy door.

It was the first time she had been in Judge Sam's apartment since the night he died.

She stopped, caught in sudden fantasy. The Saturday night before had been a dream. Judge Sam was waiting for her now, smiling, so that he wore Leigh's face, and said, "I'm going downstairs today. Because of you." He took Mari's hand with the warmth of love.

She laughed aloud, and the fantasy was gone.

Judge Sam was dead. A conspiracy of silence had settled upon that night. The brassy taste of fear was in her mouth again.

She stepped inside the apartment hesitantly, called, "Leigh, it's Mari."

There was no answer.

The wide glass wall was gray with mist. Beyond them, the ridged hills were faintly visible under their pall of yellowish haze. The blue spruce seemed to have become black sentinels in the rolling meadows.

She gave the room a swift look. The three chairs were still grouped before the fireplace. Pewter candle holders gleamed on the mantel. An empty vase was centered on the round table where she and Leigh had had their only dinner with Judge Sam.

She could almost hear his gravelly voice, saying, "Think. Think long and hard." She could almost hear him saying, "You will not be troubled again, Mari. Don't be afraid." His promise to protect her from the demon that walked through Douglass Acres.

Was that demon Ellen's restless unhappy spirit? Could it be?

Mari whispered, "No. No." And shivered, and started for the door.

A soft electric hum seemed suddenly to burn into the thick cotton silence.

She gasped, turned, trying to identify its source. It grew louder, closer.

She stood petrified, staring at the cupboard which housed Judge Sam's dumbwaiter.

The dumbwaiter. Yes. Swift and sure and unseen, rising and falling in a permanent path between this room and the kitchen below. The kitchen that looked out on the terrace, the rock garden.

She imagined someone, a face, a shadow, called here to talk to Judge Sam. They had all visited him that night, but one, arguing with him, going with him out to the balcony, perhaps to be shown the Douglass holdings, to be threatened and placated and reasoned with, all at the same time. And that faceless one, angered, despairing, had pushed the fragile man off balance, tipped his old bones over the low rail, and then ridden the dumbwaiter down, swiftly, silently, to leave Old Dandy's candle beside the broken body.

The dumbwaiter hummed to a stop.

The cupboard door opened.

Mari gasped as Arlene, her thin face stricken with terror, peered out.

"Arlene, Arlene, what on earth are you doing?" Mari rushed to help the older woman. She took the paper-weight hand in hers, and felt its trembling. She eased Arlene to the floor, to stand in stiff-legged, but shaking, defiance.

Arlene giggled. "I didn't expect to see you, Mari."

"I came to look for Leigh. I wanted to talk to him."

Arlene, voluble for the first time, said, "We were . . . I mean . . . it was a game, you see. I did it. I told Phoebe I would, and I did it. I proved I wasn't afraid. Well, you see . . ." Arlene giggled again. "Phoebe couldn't. She's just too fat to fit in. We were wondering

. . ." Arlene paused, looked guilty. "I mean, well, it sounds too silly. But we just wondered if it could be done. And the only way to find out was to try it." She stopped. "Oh, no, I went and forgot."

"Forgot what?"

"To check the time. You scared me so." She looked at her watch. "Now how long have we been talking?"

"A moment. Perhaps, two," Mari said thoughtfully. "Why does that matter?"

"You see . . ." Arlene's fingers went to her mouth. "I just wondered," she said weakly. She hobbled to the door, said breathlessly over her shoulder, "I was just proving to Phoebe that I'm not afraid."

Her thin black silhouette faded into the shadows of the hallway.

"I'm not afraid," she had said.

But Mari knew that everyone was afraid. The smiling masks covered that same alive, throbbing terror that she felt within herself.

Arlene's thin face, further shriveled with fear, seemed to float before Mari's eyes, peering from the dumbwaiter.

She and Phoebe, Mari thought, must have been wondering if someone could have substituted the dumbwaiter for the supernatural talents of Old Dandy's ghost.

But then, remembering Henley's persuasive

words, she asked herself if Arlene had been clever enough to offer one explanation to cover another. Had Arlene come to Judge Sam's rooms for some other reason?

Chapter 14

She started downstairs, her footsteps soundless on the thick rug.

The house breathed gently around her, sighed, sank and settled, its nighttime voice suddenly quite audible by day.

Within the framework of those sounds, she suddenly heard another one, a surreptitious movement, heel on wood, rustle, that followed her along the wall.

She raced to the landing, darted into the hallway, and ducked into the servants' staircase.

She collided with a fat body that cringed and shrank back. She said, "Phoebe!"

Phoebe screamed, covered her round face with her hands.

"It's me," Mari said. "Mari. Now, Phoebe, what's wrong?"

The fat hands fell away. Round gray eyes peered at Mari. "Yes. It is you, isn't it? And you scared me three quarters of the way to death, I do believe."

"I want to talk to you," Mari said soberly.

"To me? But it's television time. See? I just

slipped down for some cookies, and was slipping back up. And . . ."

But the plump fingers did not hold cookies. They were clenched around strips of stiff paper.

Phoebe saw Mari's eyes, the question in them. She put her hand behind her back. "I never liked that picture," she said defensively. "My father put it up. To remind me. It hurt, Mari. It hurt. And now he's dead . . . so I took it down yesterday, but Amantha almost caught me. I stuck it under a pillow until just now." She took a deep breath, went on in a rush, "And I have to go up to Arlene now, and . . ."

"That's what I want to talk to you about. Arlene. Arlene in the dumbwaiter, Phoebe."

"Oh. Yes. Yes, of course," Phoebe agreed. "But later. Right now . . . Arlene and I . . . there's something we have to do."

Mari put a gentle hand on Phoebe's arm. "Come along. Let's talk to Arlene together."

Phoebe, still protesting, but weakly now, waddled up the steps with her.

It was difficult for Mari to use her youth, which was her strength, to bully Phoebe, yet there seemed to be no other way. Mari was certain that the older woman knew, and was concealing, something.

Arlene, waiting at the door of the suite,

cried, "Where were you, Phoebe? I ran into Mari, and . . ." Her thin voice came to a full stop.

"Yes?" Mari demanded. "You ran into me, and what?"

Arlene and Phoebe exchanged an unreadable look.

Arlene drifted backward, slowly, into the room. Phoebe stumbled after her, and sank into an easy chair as round and as soft as she was herself.

"I thought you were Old Dandy," Phoebe said finally. "Imagine, there I am, climbing those stairs with the last of my strength, and you came at me out of the dark, from nowhere it seemed like, and . . ."

Mari said gently, "Never mind Old Dandy. Just tell me what Arlene was doing in the dumbwaiter, and what you were doing coming upstairs from the kitchen with cookies you didn't get and the shreds of a picture you certainly did get."

Phoebe opened her fat fingers wide. Shreds of stiff paper drifted down, fell like feathers on her lap.

"It was a game," Arlene said, after a long silence. "You know, Mari, we're old women. We never go anywhere, or talk to anyone. We get bored. We made up a game."

"What kind of a game?"

"Well, you see, we just wondered . . ." Arlene's voice trailed off. She looked at Phoebe.

Mari folded her hands in her lap, determined to wait, to be patient.

Phoebe sighed. "We *are* old women, Mari. I'm sixty-three. Did I tell you that? And Arlene is sixty-one."

Arlene shrilled, "That's not so, and you know it. *I'm* sixty-three. You're sixty-one."

Phoebe looked outraged.

Mari intervened. "Never mind. What were you going to say, Phoebe? About being old?"

Arlene rose, turned on the television set, fiddled with the tuner.

Phoebe gave her a pleased glance, smiled at Mari. "It's time now for Ranger Hal, dear. So if you'll excuse us?"

"No," Mari said firmly. "Now listen, you two, I want to know about this. I have to. Don't you understand?"

Phoebe sighed. "We're old women . . . we . . ." Suddenly she smiled at Mari. "It was so wonderful before. Children around the house, children, the three of them. Before the trouble began. I never thought in those days that there would be trouble."

"In spite of Old Dandy's legend?" Mari asked.

"It was a legend *then*," Phoebe answered.

"We were happy." She turned to look at Arlene. "We were happy then, weren't we? All together. Yes. All together."

Arlene nodded, braided her thin fingers.

"They were our joy," Phoebe went on dreamily. "I wish you could have seen them. Leigh, how he used to tease. And Ellen, so sweet, so sensitive. And Fern . . . a sister to the others. It was always like that. Even after Leigh and Ellen married, Fern and Ellen were so close, giggling together, sharing their little secrets. And even when poor Ellen began to fail, to shrivel and shrink, though none of us knew what was happening, even then Fern was with her, always, always. I sometimes wondered if Leigh resented . . ." Phoebe shook her head. "But no. Of course not. He was glad. They had always been like that. All together. I can see them yet. Ellen walking ahead, her hair long and dark and bound back in those braided ribbons she always wore, so graceful in her trousers. And Fern with her, hair floating like soft dark feathers in the wind, and her beautiful eyes, such beautiful eyes . . ." Phoebe folded her fat hands in her round lap. "Fern was fat then, poor child. I pitied her so. I tried to help her. But she didn't need my help. The time came when she did it herself. Better than I ever could. She's determined, Fern is. She has will power."

Arlene whined, "Phoebe, do you always have to talk about the past?"

Phoebe pushed herself up. "Mari, I must have something. I feel positively weak. I forgot those cookies, and . . ." She had opened the door as she spoke, and now she lurched back in astonishment.

Fern was there, hand raised as if to knock. She burst into laughter. "Phoebe, if you could see your face!"

"You scared me. I thought I'd go down for a snack."

"You mustn't. You'll end up too fat to walk."

Phoebe sighed.

"We were talking," Arlene said.

"About the good old days?" Fern asked. "I thought I heard somebody take my name in vain."

"You and Leigh and Ellen," Phoebe said.

"It's good to remember. But, you know, that part of our lives is over now. We have to look to the future." She smiled, her luminous eyes shining, "*We* do have to look to the future, don't we?"

That part of their lives was over, Mari thought, repeating Fern's words in her mind, but Ellen's shadow still moved through the echoing rooms of Douglass Acres, and would still move through them, until . . . until . . .

Mari suddenly wondered if Leigh were sorry he hadn't married Fern, Fern, who belonged in Douglass Acres.

Fern said, "Does anyone want a ride into Jessup? That's what I came up to find out."

The three women refused, with thanks.

Fern went on, "I think Leigh's back. I saw the other car outside."

Mari rose. "I'll go down with you."

Fern grinned, stretched, strode ahead, lithe as a cat. Phoebe whispered, "Fern?" holding out her arms. Fern laughed, went to Phoebe, hugged her in obvious pleasure. "What, Phoebe? Talking about old times, were you? I'm too old to sit on your lap now, too big and old . . ."

"Never," Phoebe told her. "Never, Fern."

Mari, following Fern downstairs, said, "You love Douglass Acres, don't you?"

"Yes. They've all been good to me. Until I came here, after my parents died, I had no place. And even before, they didn't want me." She frowned, "I never did know what happened exactly. But I can remember that much. That they didn't want me. And then they died. And Wilton, Judge Sam, brought me here."

"Do you think you'll marry Ian?"

"Phoebe keeps telling me to. She wants to see me settled down. But I don't know." Fern

210

laughed softly. "There's still some time left for me to decide. Though Phoebe doesn't think so."

Fern had come in too soon, Mari thought, as they reached the lower hallway. Phoebe had been creating a diversion with memories of the past, and she had managed to avoid explaining to Mari why Arlene had been in Judge Sam's apartment.

Fern, with a wave, went outside.

In a moment, Mari heard the car drive away.

She paused to look in the drawing room.

Amantha turned from the window with a visible start. "Oh. Oh, it's you, my dear."

"I thought Leigh might be here."

"He's gone up to the apartment, working at those papers again." Amantha sighed. "I did want to talk to you, Mari. You must, for all our sakes, persuade Leigh to give Henley the right decision, and it must be soon."

Mari opened her mouth to say that Leigh had decided. She stopped herself just in time. If Leigh hadn't told his mother, told Henley, then Mari must say nothing.

"He'll do what he thinks best, I know," she said at last.

Amantha moved her silken white hands along the carefully waved chignon. "My dear child, what is best for him, what he thinks

211

is best, that is, may not be that for all of us. Do you see?"

Mari nodded.

Amantha sighed. "The young are so selfish. What will happen if Jeff inherits? He will leave us here, unprotected, unprovided for. I am growing old. Arlene and Phoebe, poor souls, have never known the world at all. And Fern, Douglass Acres is everything to her, you know." Amantha smiled, the sweet, empty smile that was the facade behind which fear crouched, waiting. "You'll do what you can, won't you?"

"Of course," Mari told her.

She would do what she could.

But it would be for her own reasons. For Leigh's sake and hers. If that was selfish, then love must be selfish.

Jeff, wavering in the doorway, demanded, "Secrets, Amantha?"

"Jeff, do be good," she retorted smoothly.

"You, Mari?"

"No secrets that I know of, Jeff."

"Plenty of them. Ask Judge Sam."

Mari winced.

Amantha cried, "Jeff, do stop it!"

"Ask him, I said." Jeff stumbled backward. "You think we're finished with Old Dandy? I don't!"

"He doesn't know what he's saying just

now," Amantha sighed.

"But maybe he does," Mari whispered.

"Ask Judge Sam." Jeff's bloated face flushed red, then paled. "I forgot," he whispered. "I forgot Judge Sam's dead." He lurched out of the doorway, climbed the steps breathing heavily.

From the upper floor, Mari heard Jeff's, "Hey, Leigh, where you going in such a hurry? What you doing? Hey, hold on a minute, Leigh. You better take Mari and run. Listen to me, Old Dandy's coming back."

The voice, magnified by the stairwell, sent a strange quiver of fright through Mari.

Then Leigh appeared at the top of the steps. He came down, running.

Mari put out her hand, a hopeful smile at her lips. It faded when she saw his face. He looked gaunt, frozen. He seemed not to see her until she said his name. Then he glanced at her, brushed by. "Not now, Mari." He went outside.

Moments later, she heard the car pull away.

"How odd," Amantha said, and withdrew behind the draped double doors of her suite.

Mari sighed. She went back upstairs to the suite in the north wing. She hoped, that time, to be able to talk to Phoebe and Arlene without interruption.

She tapped at the door, and Phoebe quavered, "Who is it now?"

Mari went in. "Just me."

Phoebe and Arlene sat on the sofa, hand in hand. They eyed her in obvious suspicion. The television set was turned off.

Mari said, "You never told me what you were really doing upstairs, Arlene."

Arlene didn't answer.

Phoebe sighed. Her round gray eyes sparkled with sudden tears. "Mari, do you know . . . we just want you and Leigh to be happy, to be safe."

Astonished, Arlene shrilled, "Just a minute, Phoebe."

But Phoebe went on, "We do, Mari. We do. You see, Arlene lost her sweetheart . . . in that war, I told you. And I . . . well, I wasn't quite candid with you, Mari. I couldn't be. Judge Sam wouldn't let me. He said . . ."

"That's enough," Arlene yelled. "Now, Phoebe, about the dumbwaiter, why don't you . . ."

"I was in love once. Yes. Twenty-six years ago. The man was married, you see." Phoebe's face had grown thin, pale. "I should have known better. I was the older by ten years. Not young and foolish. Just old and foolish, I guess. But he had such beautiful eyes. I

214

. . . I had a baby, Mari. My father took the infant from my arms, and gave it away. And I came home. The man, his wife, were gone. I never saw them again."

Mari, her throat tight with quick sympathy, whispered, "Oh, Phoebe, the picture . . ."

"Yes. He put it up to remind me. And I took it down. I took it down so I could forget."

Phoebe's mouth twisted. "It is a long way around to explain that . . ."

"Tell her," Arlene said insistently. "That's enough of that, Phoebe."

"Yes. Enough." Phoebe smiled faintly. "You see, in this house, love is never safe. Never. Arlene and I . . . we know that. So . . . so we decided to find out, Mari. If we could, who . . ."

"You were playing detective?" Mari asked incredulously, "Arlene was timing the dumbwaiter trip?"

"It seemed so logical," Phoebe said.

"But it was a game, too," Arlene insisted. "I told you, Mari, I was proving to Phoebe that I'm not afraid."

"Let it go, Arlene." Phoebe went on, speaking to Mari. "I guess it was silly of us. Two old women who have lived so long with make-believe, trying to discover secrets that shouldn't be discovered."

"But you mustn't," Mari cried, her eyes

burning with tears. "Don't you see? It might be dangerous."

"Living is dangerous," Phoebe said with a smile, a smile that didn't wipe the fear from her round gray eyes.

And Arlene asked, "Mari, couldn't you just go away?"

Chapter 15

It was only when Mari had returned to the emptiness of her room that she began to wonder if Phoebe and Arlene had managed cleverly to deceive her. If, by pretending to be scatterbrained old women, they had distracted her from seeing a truth almost within her vision. Did they want her safety? Was that why they asked her to leave Douglass Acres? Or were they hiding a deep jealousy of love? One that had led them step by step to shared madness, to shared murder?

Wilton, Ellen, Judge Sam . . .

Mari sighed. Questions. No answers.

But one thing she knew. Phoebe and Arlene, since the day of the effigy, had changed. Since the moment, two days before, when Mari had run screaming into the hallway . . .

Now she went to the window. It seemed to her that her world had shrunk until it existed only within the narrow bounds of the yellowish hills in the distance and the smudged rose brick of the big house.

The overcast had thinned. Beyond it, she guessed, there would be sun, for the day had taken on a strange coppery glare that stung her eyes. Or was that the effect of gathering tears waiting to be wept?

She turned away impatiently. She would not cry. She reminded herself how, with each change of school, she had been fearful, but how she had always managed to make a place for herself. She must do the same in Douglass Acres. She could not share Leigh with a memory wife, so she must lay Ellen's lingering spirit to rest. She must finally unmask Judge Sam's demon.

She sighed again. Questions. No answers.

But the note long overdue now to Susie was still unwritten.

That was one thing Mari could do. She sat at the desk. The greeting, Dear Susie, was simple. But after that what? Mari asked herself. Dear Susie, I'm terribly afraid . . . afraid for my marriage, afraid for my life . . .

In the end, Mari settled for a kind of short-hand. "Trip fine, beautiful place, hope all is well, more later, love . . ."

She put the note into an envelope, addressed it, feeling as if she had done a hard day's work.

"Lovey, will you be going far?" Nellie asked. The small woman was up on a ladder before the kitchen cupboard. She dragged out a pot, passed it down to Mari.

218

"Just outside. I thought I'd paint for a little while."

"Good. I'll be right here if you want me."

Mari thanked her, a question in her tilted eyes.

"It's a dread day. You'll see when you go out. Red sun hiding somewhere, and hell's heat gathering." Nellie came down the ladder. "But I'll be right here."

Mari went out of doors, considering Nellie's oblique warning.

The brick walls of the house kept it cool, even chilled. But outside the thick, damp heat took Mari's breath away. And the coppery glare was even stronger. Red sun hiding, and hell's heat gathering, she thought.

She arranged the palette, the pad on her knees. She settled herself facing the yellow hills, which in the strange light seemed to glow. She remembered thinking when she first came that she would learn to love the weird empty landscape because it was the soil from which Leigh had sprung, and through it, she would know him. She wondered, now, if that would ever be possible. For the Leigh who had brushed by her earlier on the steps had not been the Leigh she married.

Her hand moved the brush from palette to pad, free to do with color and line whatever it wanted. She, determined to put her wits to work, tried to remember what Judge Sam had said when she blurted out the thing that had been done in her room. She recalled the gravelly mumble, "Should I have known? Or have I always known? Did I willfully close my eyes . . . ?"

To what could Judge Sam have willfully closed his jet black eyes?

A sudden sound made Mari leap with fright.

Jonah said cheerfully, "It's just me, and looking at the nicest sight I ever laid eyes on."

She smiled tremulously. "I was thinking."

"I haven't made a pretty girl like you jump so in thirty years." He shoved back his peaked cap, gave a tug to his red-checked vest. "Makes me feel good."

She noticed then that he had an easel under his arm. He saw her looking at it, and set it down.

"For me, Jonah?"

"I'm told that you know what to do with this bundle of sticks. I don't, but if you tell me, I'll help you stand it up, if it stands up, that is."

"Oh, it does. But where did you get it?"

"From the general store, believe it or not, and I might as well tell you, you've set Old Ned up for a year. Why, since I took you in there, he's been walking around with his chest out two inches further than it can go."

Jonah grinned. "And now he's sore he didn't think of it himself. But Leigh was in, asking, and between them, they found it. Leigh asked me to bring it out to you."

"Leigh did? Oh, Jonah, isn't that wonderful?" The sudden warmth she felt made her want to sing, to dance.

"You can stand something wonderful for a change," Jonah said.

With her showing him how it was to be done, he got the easel up, adjusted it to stand evenly among the rocks. Then, though she protested, he brought her a chair from the kitchen.

"Go on," he said. "Try it."

She sat down. "Perfect."

He crouched down at her feet, his wizened face suddenly sober. "What's Leigh up to, prowling all over town, first to Henley, then the older folks?"

"I don't know, Jonah."

"Something anyhow." Then, "I figured you'd be gone out of this place for good by now, Mari."

"Did you?"

"It wouldn't hurt."

"It would hurt Leigh. And me."

"Could be worse this way, though."

"Yes," she whispered. "It could be, Jonah."

He gave her a thoughtful look. "The old

221

man, he used to say Old Dandy's ghost was good."

She nodded.

"Then how come Old Dandy's light was always talked about, here, in Jessup, I mean, and was never seen? Not by human eyes anyhow. Not until . . . well, it was maybe thirteen or fourteen years ago. And that's when I marked the trouble starting."

"Thirteen or fourteen years ago? But what happened then?"

"Fern got knocked off a horse, banged her head good. They found her, Leigh did, that is, with the candle beside her, and her out cold. Not hurt real bad, but it was a scare."

"And then?"

"Other things, small, but they grew, they grew to be big. Like a valance that fell on my Nellie. There was a candle then, too. And one time, when Amantha had pneumonia, she woke up to see a candle burning at her feet. Not nice, that wasn't, to scare her so. And the night Wilton died . . ."

"I see," Mari said.

But she wasn't sure exactly what she did see. The legend of Old Dandy had existed through generations in Douglass Acres, but his candle hadn't begun to gleam, until . . . until what? A half-thought flickered and faded in her mind. There was something she ought to remember. Something important, but it evaded her.

She looked at Jonah, but saw, beyond his shoulder, in a window of the north wing, Phoebe's face peering down at her.

Had Phoebe been trying to help?

Mari asked, "Jonah, did you ever hear that Phoebe had a sweetheart?"

He grinned, "Hushed up good, but true enough. Phoebe never had a chance either. The man had a harridan of a wife. And Judge Sam moved him out of here pretty quick. Judge Sam was mighty particular." Jonah shook his head. "And if you think that's wrong, it's because you're still young." He climbed to his feet. "I better let you get on with your painting, and I better get me back to town."

Mari asked if he would mail her letter to Susie.

"Sure." He glanced at the envelope. "Paris. I saw it once, back in the first war." He grinned. "Never got back, though I sure meant to."

Mari thanked him for bringing the easel, said goodbye, and watched him bound into the kitchen, his short bowed legs working like pistons.

She turned back to her painting.

Phoebe, she knew, was still at the window.

Phoebe had had a sweetheart long before. Perhaps, as she had said, she wanted Mari to be safe. Perhaps the playing of detective had been sincere, and Arlene's visit to Judge Sam's apartment on the dumbwaiter simply as she claimed.

Thirteen or fourteen years before small tricks had begun, small tricks with Old Dandy's candle. . . .

Judge Sam had said, "Was I blind? Should I have known? Did I willfully close my eyes?"

Mari was certain that he had known about those small tricks, recognized the demon, as he called it. Could he have assumed, wanted to assume, that the candles left near Wilton and Ellen's bodies, were two more small tricks? It seemed hardly possible, yet, if it were someone he wanted to protect . . .

Mari shook her head. No. Judge Sam would not protect a murderer. But Wilton's death had seemed an accident. And Ellen's was suicide. Or, had the warning to Mari convinced the old man of the rightness of long-held suspicions?

The brush moved slowly under her hand. The browns and blues took shape slowly. Her bent head was golden in the copper glare, her small face absorbed, as the browns feathered into two crouching cats, blue eyes shining, aloof, Susie's cats, tails curled, whiskers bristling, backs arched. Susie's cats . . .

The yellowish hills were gone. Mari sat on the windowsill of the apartment. The cats pranced delicately among the china cups, while Susie smiled indulgently, a permissive mother, who would shout a warning ten seconds too late.

Mari didn't hear Leigh come up behind her. She didn't know how long he'd been there before he said, suddenly at her shoulder, "That's better than sitting on the ground, isn't it?"

She started, a quiver quickly subdued.

But not quickly enough. Leigh said, "It's as if you're strung on wire, Mari."

"I was concentrating," she said.

"No. It's more than that."

The glare was so intense it was hard to see his face.

"The easel is wonderful, Leigh. I was so surprised."

He said absently, "Those are Susie's cats, aren't they?"

"That's what came up. I intended to paint the hills."

"But the cats came up instead."

"It's funny how that works sometimes."

"Not to me. You'd sooner be there than here. And I don't blame you." He waved her quick protest away. "Never mind, Mari."

Then, "I wanted to ask you, were you up in Judge Sam's apartment this morning?"

She gave him. a surprised look "Yes, I was, for just a minute."

"What were you looking for?"

"You."

"Me?"

She held herself steady under his searching look. "I wanted to talk to you about . . . about everything."

"I'm sorry." He paused. "I'm sorry I had to hurry away earlier. It was important that I see Henley right away. I'll be going back into Jessup again after dinner."

"We don't have much time together, do we?" she said softly.

"But we do have *now*."

"Then . . ."

But he cut in, "Darling, do you know what I really want?" His hand settled under her small chin, tilted her face up. "I'd like to see you smile."

The terror of the day past fell away, a burden slipping from her narrow shoulders, welded chains suddenly melting into air.

The smile that glowed like sunlight on her face was real, free. He bent, touched his lips lightly to hers. Then he moved back. "Go on now. Make use of the easel. I'm going to sit here, watch you, the way I did that day in

Amsterdam. Remember?"

"Yes, I remember." Still smiling, she took up the brush.

They talked, while the cats changed character under her moving hand, became gay rather than aloof. They talked of Munich, and choucroute garni and Paris and Susie and Copenhagen and Tivoli's blossoming white lilacs.

She painted, listening to his deep voice, answering him, and forgot to be afraid.

She forgot that she once suspected he had married her, brought her to Douglass Acres, because he knew he must have a wife. She forgot that she had wondered if he wished he had chosen Fern instead. She forgot the sweet smiling masks that made her an intruder in the home to which he had brought her.

She became light-headed with joy, laughing with it, beautiful with it.

And then, with the copper glare fading into shadows, Leigh said, "We'd better go in now."

"But I hate for it to end."

"I have something to do." His face was suddenly grim.

Had he really been smiling before? she asked herself.

He took the easel and chair. She gathered her paints.

The house seemed to be wreathed in coppery clouds. She looked at it, then at Leigh, her joy gone. Had he wanted to be with her, just to be with her? Had he been watching her? Or had he been protecting her?

She wore red again, hoping that this time he would notice it. A brilliant red blouse, sleeveless, and snug, with a V-cut neck, and a wide, pleated skirt that emphasized her tiny waist. She found the Chanel No. 5 that Leigh had bought her in Paris, a huge flacon, which she, protesting his extravagance, had never opened. She did so now, dabbed it behind her ears, at her throat.

She went through the ritual of preparation, trying to recall the joy of her hour with Leigh, but it had become no more than a sweet memory. The menace of Douglass Acres reclaimed her.

At last, she forced herself to go downstairs.

Jeff, Ian, and Leigh were in the drawing room with Geraldine. Fern soon joined them.

Mari wished that Leigh would smile at her in the old way. She needed to see again the glowing warmth that had once made her feel like Eve, like the only women in the world.

Instead, he seemed to have forgotten those good moments on the terrace. He was watching Fern.

She wore a pale green shirt, green trousers

the same shade. Her long hair was bound in a green braided ribbon. She had style, a compelling quality, Mari decided. It was no wonder that she drew Leigh's eyes, that Ian was so attentive.

Fern said, "Jeff was telling me that he was going to talk you into giving him some money, Leigh. For going back into the auto business. Our big financier, Jeff."

The big blond man rumbled a wordless protest into his glass.

Leigh said, "It might not be a bad idea."

"Judge Sam will turn in his grave," Fern answered.

"You could mind your own business," Geraldine flared, her narrowed eyes suddenly glittering.

Fern's oval white face stiffened. Her luminous gray eyes dulled. "I *am* sorry. I forgot I don't have the right to give an opinion."

Mari felt an instant rush of sympathy. She knew what it was to be unwanted, to be an outsider.

But it was Ian who said, "That's not how Geraldine meant it, Fern."

Leigh looked at his watch. Then his dark, veiled glance returned to Fern.

Mari realized then that he had bean watching the time, off and on, all afternoon. Out on the terrace. Here in the drawing room. She

229

wondered what he was waiting for. She decided that he must be looking forward to his after-dinner appointment with Henley.

Nellie came in, breaking the silence that had fallen, to say that dinner was ready.

It was an ordeal, Mari thought, to be gotten through as quickly as possible, and made worse by the pretense that all was well.

Amantha, perfectly groomed, her white waves smooth, smiled sweetly, said, "It's been a lovely day, hasn't it?"

Phoebe and Arlene chimed an obedient agreement.

The sweet smiling masks were firmly in place. But Mari sensed the fear behind them.

Leigh, with a glance at his watch, excused himself, and left for Jessup.

Mari, with the others, went into the drawing room.

There Nellie served them coffee from a big silver pot.

Though the lamp lights were on, the pale mist seemed to have thickened in the room.

Mari caught a glimpse of herself in the old mirror over the mantel. She looked strange, hardly recognizable, her mouth twisted, her eyes narrowed. She shuddered at the distortions.

She remembered that she had once thought of the Douglass women as being predatory birds, and studied them now, and then dismissed the fantasy as being a diversion that would never help her understand why someone wanted to drive her away from Douglass Acres, why Ellen's spirit would not rest.

Phoebe and Arlene retired, arguing, as usual, about the nightly television ritual.

Geraldine, followed by Jeff, bottle under his arm, left without a good night.

Amantha yawned, patted her mouth, and withdrew.

Fern, Ian, and Mari remained together.

But Mari noticed that Fern was restless, pacing the floor, as graceful as a restless cat, and that Ian, smiling gently, was trying to divide his attention between Fern and herself.

She had hoped to wait until Leigh's return from Jessup, but realized that Fern and Ian might want some time alone together.

She waited for the right moment, then, with a peculiar feeling of disappointment, she left them.

She supposed, as she climbed the dim stairway, that she had been preparing herself all day for something to happen, for that something to happen which might bring to an end the suspense in which she waited. But the day was nearly ended. Her dance of fear must continue.

She hesitated, as had become habitual to her, before her door. She glanced along the hallway. The green velour settee was in place. The usual mellow, meaningless voices rippled along the walls from the suite at the end of the wing. At least Phoebe and Arlene were settled for the night.

Mari sighed, wished that Leigh had returned. She thrust the door open and went in.

The room was golden with light. The window drapes drawn back, so that the glass was a dark empty rectangle, reflecting her white face and red dress as clearly as a mirror.

Chapter 16

There was something wrong. Instinct told her.

A cloak of fright enwrapped her. She stood very still, frozen against the door, waiting. Nothing happened.

Her eyes moved from her rigid reflection in the window. They sought the hearth, moved to the mantel, shifted quickly across the room to the dressing table, the closets, the chest, then, finally, to the bed.

Leigh's tan and brown spread was neat, unwrinkled, untouched since he had moved up to Judge Sam's apartment two days before.

Nellie had been in. For Mari's bed had been prepared for the night, sheet carefully folded back.

But, on its puffed pillow, centered neatly, nestling like a diamond in a velvet jewel box, lay a gun.

Mari's throat went dry with panic. Her hand went to her mouth, stifling a scream. Her sense of expectation had been right.

Judge Sam's demon had walked through Douglass Acres once again.

The gun, symbol of death, of violence,

seemed black in the golden light.

She went to it, taking small hesitant steps, her hands balled into small fists. She had never actually seen a gun before, certainly never touched one. She peered at it, loathing it, not for what it was, but for what it could do.

She wondered why it had been left on her pillow. Was she to be driven to madness, to suicide, like Ellen? Or was it meant, like the disarray of her room, the pink scrawled message, to send her into flight from Leigh, from Douglass Acres?

She reached out a hand to touch the gun, then drew back. She retreated to the big leather chair, Leigh's chair, seeking comfort by curling up inside its wide arms.

She watched the gun on the pillow, waiting for it somehow to give the demon's plan away.

It grew late. The house settled into its nighttime song.

As she crouched there, rigid, cold, it slowly came to her that Leigh must not know about the gun.

Or did he already know? Had he gone upstairs before he left for Jessup? Had he put the gun on her pillow, put it there for her to find? Did she know Leigh?

Her eyes stung with tears. She fought her insidious doubts. No. Not Leigh. Not her love.

He did not know about the gun. And he must not.

She saw it quite clearly. If he knew, he would send her away. He would see the threat, and try to save her from it. He had not wanted to bring her here because he didn't want her to know of the memories that tormented him. He had suggested she leave as soon as he realized that those things he once believed Ellen had done herself had actually been done by someone else. He wanted to protect Mari. And if she left him now, left him in Douglass Acres, it would mean the end of their life together.

Her eyes searched the room. There must be someplace in which she could hide the gun. Somewhere no one could ever find it.

She must thwart the demon's purpose. If the gun were to be used to kill her, she must prevent it. If it were to be used to drive her mad, she must stay sane. If it were to frighten Leigh, he must never see it.

She crouched in the chair, waiting. She was patient now, her mind quite made up. Finally, with the house silent around her, she rose. She approached the bed gingerly.

She ducked down beside the pillow and, wincing, put out her hand in a quick, blind movement. When nothing happened, she forced her fingers to close around the barrel. Holding it carefully, she got to her feet.

Phoebe and her picture were in her mind.

Hardly daring to breathe, she went to the door, eased it open.

The hallway was silent, filled with its ever-present shadows.

She listened for long, long moments before she moved on tiptoe toward the green settee which made a thicker shadow against the wall.

It was the only place, the closest place, she could think of. She must slide it under the pillow quickly, quickly return to her room.

But the pillow stuck. She couldn't move it with one hand. She put the gun on the rug. She tugged at the pillow with both hands. It came up with a rush, a whisper of resistant fabric. She reached for the gun.

The wheel-shaped chandelier suddenly blazed with light, casting weird dancing shadows on the wall before her.

Jeff, on the steps, demanded hoarsely, "What in the hell are you doing with Judge Sam's gun?"

His booming voice went echoing along the hallway.

She whispered, "Wait, Jeff. Let me tell you . . ."

But he, wavering up the last few steps of the staircase, shouted, "We've had enough trouble here. If you want to kill yourself go some place else to do it!"

"But I wasn't . . ." she cried.

She rose, backed against the wall, suddenly at bay.

"Then what are you doing?"

"I found it. I wanted to hide it."

"You found it where?"

"In my room."

"A man can't even go down to get himself a drink in his own house without seeing . . ." He shook his head. "Mari, you must be crazy." His bloodshot eyes stared into hers. "Crazy, like Ellen . . . that's what it is."

"Please, Jeff, don't tell . . ."

But even as the words left her lips, she realized that it was too late.

Leigh had come down the stairs from the apartment above. He was staring at her, his face white, his eyes shadowed. Amantha, in a blue dressing gown, her white hair arranged into two heavy braids, stood just behind Jeff. Phoebe and Arlene, leaning together as if for support, pressed against the green settee. Fern, with a book in her hand, frowned from beyond Amantha's shoulder. Nellie whispered softly, "It's Old Dandy again."

Mari was aware of all of them. But she spoke to Leigh alone. "I just didn't want you to know about it. I thought I would hide it."

"You were in Judge Sam's apartment this

morning," Leigh said slowly. "Is that what you were looking for then?"

She shook her head.

Amantha said, "Why, my poor child, why should you want to do such a terrible thing? Have we not welcomed you with open arms?"

"But what?" Mari asked desperately, "Do what?"

Geraldine answered. "Why, of course, we understand, Mari. You were going to . . ." She turned to Leigh. "You must have Dr. Bender in."

"No, no," Mari cried.

But Leigh, his face grim, yet somehow turned away from hers, took the gun, said, "Mari, I want you to go into your room. I want you to pack your things immediately. I'm going to take you away from here the first thing in the morning."

"You'll take me away from here," she repeated, bewildered, shaken, by his tone.

Amantha cried, "My dear boy, you mustn't do that!"

"Leigh, we need you," Fern said, crowding into the circle around Mari.

Still not quite looking at her, he told her, "Mari, you've been very brave. I can't subject you to this harassment any more. I see what's happening to you."

"But, Leigh, I wasn't going to shoot myself!

I was hiding the gun. Why else would I put it under the pillow?"

"Or, having put it there earlier, why would you be taking it out?" Jeff demanded.

"You were upstairs this morning, Mari. Remember? You told me so yourself," Leigh said.

Her eyes went to Arlene. Arlene had been there, too. Was the gun what Arlene had been looking for? Had she, interrupted by Mari, gone back there later?

"I didn't know Judge Sam had a gun," Mari whispered.

"But who could have put it in your room," Geraldine asked.

"Somebody. Anybody." Even to Mari that sounded lame.

But Phoebe said, "I heard something in the hallway. Before we came down for dinner." She turned to Arlene. "Didn't we hear somebody?"

"You?" Fern laughed. "You two wouldn't hear a bomb go off. Not with your television set on and blasting all the time."

"But we did," Phoebe said. "We did," she told Leigh.

"I'll take you away, Mari. First thing in the morning," Leigh told her. "Now do as I say. Go in and pack."

Mari retreated, wordless now. The circle

broke open for her. She edged into her room.

She heard Jeff say, "First smart thing Leigh's done in years, isn't it, Geraldine?" and Geraldine's, "If he wants his wife sane, it is. Or wants her at all."

Mari waited, leaning against the door, until the voices faded away, until the house once again sank into stillness.

Then she went in search of Leigh.

Her eyes, her throat, burned with unshed tears. She could hardly speak when she found him on the floor below. He was on the telephone. "Long distance," he said. "Boston. Red Eagle Charter Service. They'll have a special night number." He heard Mari then, turned to look at her, and shook his head.

"Leigh, you must wait until I can explain."

He spoke into the phone. "All right. Connect me." Then, briefly, he made the arrangements for the charter plane to fly in to Jessup the following morning.

She listened, trembling. A shadow fell across the wall opposite. She spun around, looking for its source. There was no one behind her, but the drawing room door seemed ajar. She went toward it.

Leigh said, "Mari, just a minute."

She turned back.

He had completed the call, put down the

phone. Now he said, "Please do what I tell you."

She started to speak. He touched her lips with his fingers. "Not now." She turned wearily to go upstairs.

Fern, luminous eyes cold, demanded, "How can you do it, Mari? This is where Leigh belongs. How can you take him away?"

"I can't . . ."

"Do something," Fern retorted. "Why don't you do something?"

Leigh, with grim amusement, asked, "And just what do you propose that Mari do?"

Mari didn't wait to hear Fern's answer. She ran up the steps, fled down the hallway under the weird dancing shadows of the chandelier.

Nellie, waiting in the room, said, "Lovey, maybe it's for the best."

"It isn't. Leigh will always be sorry. He loves it here. It's his home, and his responsibility. Judge Sam understood that. If Leigh gives it up for me, he'll never forgive me, Nellie. And I'll never forgive myself."

"Lovey, sooner unforgiven and alive, than mourned and dead!"

"Nellie!"

"It is best, lovey." The older woman rubbed her hands briskly together. "Now let me see, where to begin? I'll pack for you. I'll get you set for an early start."

"No, Nellie, thanks. I'll do it myself."

"I'll go on then. Pack and get some rest, lovey. And dream of you and Leigh in some new place."

"But you think he should stay here, Nellie."

"I think he must do what he must." She gave Mari a warm smile, and went out.

Mari sank to the edge of the bed. Through a mist of tears, she looked helplessly around the room, not knowing where to begin. Finally, she shook her head. She could not give up, she would not.

The tears held back for so long finally came. She let herself be carried away by the sweet release of stormy weeping.

Later, calmed, exhausted, she got up, turned off the light. She curled up in Leigh's chair.

She thought that if she and Leigh had not met in April sunlight in Amsterdam, he would have returned someday alone to Douglass Acres. But they had met, married. He came home with a new wife. One who stood in the way of the past, offered him the future, instead. He had come home, dreading his memories. Someone had known of those memories, exploited them. Someone who hoped to drive Mari away, or drive her mad, or drive her to her death.

Suddenly she felt strong, exultant. Leigh

loved her. He was going to leave Douglass Acres with her. Ellen's shadow would no longer be between them.

Leigh loved her.

Then who hates me? she asked herself. Jeff and Geraldine because I stand between them and the control they want of this house? Amantha, who has hidden herself in books since Wilton died, because I am Leigh's wife? Phoebe and Arlene? Did Arlene take the gun from Judge Sam's apartment? Why had she and Phoebe seemed to shrivel and age when they found out about the effigy? Why should the two old ladies hate her, Mari asked herself. Because I know love and they never have? But they have known love, both of them. Fern? Mari imagined Fern's oval face, her long dark hair held back by a braided ribbon. Fern. Mari remembered Phoebe describing Fern as she had been years before, fat, clumsy, with dark hair like feathers blowing in the wind, and Ellen, hair long, hair dark . . . Mari straightened up.

It was Ellen who had worn her hair bound in a braided ribbon. Ellen who wore pants. Ellen . . . slim, tall. Why had Fern copied Ellen's style? Was it because she loved Ellen so much? Or was it to remind Leigh, to make him fall in love with her, to claim him for her own? Had Leigh given that strange hurt

243

cry when he first saw Fern because he had mistaken her for Ellen? Had Fern changed herself for Leigh, only to have him marry someone else before he saw her again? Mari got to her feet.

She paced the floor. She was remembering now what Jonah had told her. The first time Old Dandy's candle had been seen was fourteen years before, when Fern was knocked off a horse. She would have been about twelve then, feeling an outsider, needing attention Had she begun to light the candles in those days, continued the prank until it was a prank no more?

Could Fern have sent the cable which brought Leigh back to Douglass Acres? Fern who tried to drive Mari away? Had Fern killed Judge Sam? Was she the demon from whom the old man had vowed to protect Mari.

Now Mari conjured up Fern's face again, searching the imagined contours with her artist's eyes. She found no evidence to support her sudden intuition, yet everything she knew seemed to fit together, to fit and not quite fit.

A damp breeze whispered at the window, touched her hot cheeks. She returned to Leigh's chair to sit down.

She felt that she had the answer. But she didn't know what to do, how to prove it.

Perhaps, in the morning, she could ask for Leigh's help. The night hours slowly faded, and with them went her hope. For soon, soon it would be too late.

In those pale moments just before dawn, the time of sick dreams and terror, she heard a sudden rattle at the window.

She struggled out of the chair, stood waiting.

The sound came again, identifiable then. A handful of pebbles bouncing off the glass.

She thought it was Leigh, signaling to her.

She darted to the window.

Old Dandy's candle flickered in the masked gray shadows below.

Chapter 17

Old Dandy's candle was once more alight in Douglass Acres.

Mari stared at it in fascinated horror. It seemed to her that she saw the beckoning hand of death. She wanted to live, to live.

But it was true, as Phoebe had once said, life had its dangers.

She whispered, "Leigh," as if his name were a prayer. She turned from the window, crossed the room, kicking off her shoes as she went. She eased the door open, listened for a still moment, then slipped into the hallway.

She knew the house now. She was quicker than the last time she had gone racing downstairs through the waiting shadows.

She must discover the truth. For Leigh.

The kitchen door was open. She slipped through it into the silent emptiness of the terrace. The candle was gone. She stared at the place she had last seen it, not believing what her eyes told her.

The light was gone.

She took a deep breath, and set out to search the courtyard. The rocks were cold, dew-wet, sharp-edged. She stepped gingerly, trying for silence, so that she could listen for, hear, another step nearby. The step of Judge Sam's demon.

The house loomed above her, its windows blank. A dawn breeze whispered at its eaves and wings.

Mari, squinting into the shadows, suddenly saw the light again. It flickered near Old Dandy's underground room.

She wanted to turn, to run away. But the candle beckoned her on. She had to know. She went toward it cautiously, listening.

It grew brighter and brighter. She saw nothing but the light, heard nothing but the wind. One step, then another. She waited breathlessly for something to happen.

When it did, when she heard the sound behind her and tried, too late, to turn, she was struck down.

There was just the sound, her own half-response, and a quick terrible blow that exploded against her head. She fell into instant unconsciousness.

It lasted, it seemed to Mari, only moments before it was ripped apart by a raw wedge of throbbing pain that brought her to partial awareness.

She lay still, unmoving. She sensed someone near, and knew the threat, but was unable to protect herself.

Strong hands grasped her at the shoulders, jerked and rolled and pulled her along the gravel in quick hard hitches of movement.

A dozen small cuts stabbed through her frozen flesh. There was blood in her mouth. Thin lights flickered beneath her closed eyelids. She heard her rasping breath.

The spin of terror slowed. The hands disappeared.

Mari gathered her strength to scream, to fight. But the hands returned. They grabbed her, gave a single hard push.

The earth fell away from below her. She tumbled headlong down a flight of wooden steps, and landed, sprawling, with her cheek pressed into a damp earthen floor.

A few quick thuds, wooden steps creaking.

Closer to consciousness now, she knew she was cornered. She waited for the moment which would give her a chance of survival, hoarding the meager resources of her strength.

She listened to the moving footsteps, the hard, quick pantings of effort.

"There. There. That's right. Now let me see."

It was the voice of Judge Sam's demon. It was Fern.

The recognition was a white light within the dulled center of Mari's mind. Fern. Yes.

Yes. It had all fit, hadn't it?

"Let's see. Fall down the steps and hit head. That first. Back on stairs then."

The hands gave a quick pull. Pain brought the shadows back. Mari was flung one way, then another, limp, lost.

A pause then.

"Yes. Right." Fern's voice was cold, brittle. "A blonde little doll. How could I know it would happen that way?"

Mari pieced it together. She knew that Fern was setting a stage, props for a scene to be played. But Mari did not dare open her eyes, lest some faint light glimmer in them and give her away, and hasten whatever it was that Fern was planning.

"Her own fault," Fern murmured. "Fell down the steps first. Bruise on back of head accounted for. Then shot herself. What she had come here for. Hand on gun, yes, in fingers."

Mari saw it very clearly now. She would lie in the dark, but somewhere nearby, Old Dandy's candle would burn.

She would be found, blood-smeared, self-destroyed, a second Ellen. Another burden that Leigh would never be able to lay down.

"Her fault," Fern whispered. "Now. Now."

She bent over Mari, reached for her hand,

the gun ready to be pressed into Mari's fingers, the trigger to be pulled, the final escape to be made.

But the moments of quiescence were over. On the swift current of her hoarded strength, Mari rose, heaved to her knees, flailing with both fists.

Fern, larger, heavier, seized her. Mari broke free, only to fall again under Fern's weight.

The gun was between them now, bruising, cutting. The silent terrible struggle seemed to go on forever. But it ended. At last it ended.

A hard muffled explosion slapped at the damp walls, and acrid odor spilled into Mari's throat. At the same time, there was light, a blinding light that sent disturbed spiders running along the wet walls to the slit window.

Mari froze with Fern pressed against her.

They leaned together, swaying, as though in a grotesque dance, while beyond them, their swollen shadows mimicked their slow steps.

There was the blinding light, the drunken shadows, and Fern's white face.

There was the shout, pounding footsteps, Leigh's sobbed, "Oh, God, no, please," and Ian's, "Fern, don't!"

Mari knew that the spiders had fled at the coming of the torch. She knew that the two men had seemed to fall from the ceiling when they leaped the steps into the room.

But the muffled explosion still echoed through her. She still felt the gun, held between her chest and Fern's. She still stared into Fern's luminous, hate-filled eyes, unable to turn away.

Then Fern stepped back. A great gout of blood blackened her shirt. The gun slipped from her fingers. She fell in stumbling slow motion, hands pressed to the gaping wound in her chest. She lay still, wide gray eyes aglow with hate, a faint smile on her moving lips.

The nightmare moments came to an end when Leigh gathered Mari close to him, whispering words of reassurance she didn't hear, for Fern was saying, "Her fault. The blonde doll's fault."

Ian said gently, "Be quiet, Fern. I'll get Dr. Bender."

She turned her head, coughed. A thin trickle of blood ran from the corner of her mouth. "Dr. Bender to mend me? No. No."

But Ian raced up the steps, and soon Mari heard pounding through the courtyard.

"Poor Ian. He knew. It's why he came around. He used me. I used him." A shudder moved through her long slim body. "And now a doctor to mend me." She moved her hands on her chest.

Mari read the gesture. Within the circle of Leigh's arms she stirred. He seemed to understand. Together, they drew closer to Fern. They kneeled beside her.

"Yes, Leigh," she whispered. "Ellen. Ian knew in his heart. He was waiting. He tried to blame you, Leigh, and couldn't believe it. I know. I know. And ended pretending, to all of you, to me, so that I . . . so I . . . Yes, Ellen. My way, though. Before that, Wilton, Wilton . . ." Fern turned her head from side to side. "It hurts," she moaned. "It hurts, Leigh."

"Be still," he said. "Rest."

"Rest?" She gave a hoarse chuckle. It brought more blood to her lips.

Mari whispered, "Please . . . please, Fern."

"The blonde doll is full of pity. I don't deserve it. Ellen, Wilton, Judge Sam . . ." Fern grimaced, "Before that, my father?"

"Your father, Fern?"

"No, no. That was my mother, I guess. My mother did it, and I was left alone. Yes, that's how it was. Judge Sam was sorry for me then. He brought me to Douglass Acres. I was his responsibility, he said. I never knew why. But that's what he said. I was his responsibility, but there was my bad blood, you know. He was sorry for me, but not sorry enough to let me love you, Leigh. That's all I ever

252

wanted. To love you, to belong to Douglass Acres. But it was Wilton who kept me from you. So I left Old Dandy's candle burning. I did it before, a lot of times, when I was a kid. Maybe for fun, maybe to get even because I wasn't a Douglass. But I left Old Dandy's candle burning here. After a few nights, he came to see. I was waiting, with a rock. Nobody knew he didn't fall on the broken step. But you married Ellen anyway. Leigh, you shouldn't have done that." Bitterness drained the agony from Fern's words. "Poor Ellen, weak, so weak."

"She begged me to take her away," Leigh said softly. "She begged me, and I told her she was safer in her home than anywhere else. She told me then that I didn't want to leave you, Fern. And the next day she was dead."

"Yes. The next day she was dead. I had told her we'd been lovers since childhood, and she believed me. I told her we'd kept on, even after you married her."

Leigh made a sound, a grunt of pain. Mari pressed closer to him, offering silent comfort.

Fern was saying, "I poisoned Wimpy, and ripped Ellen's gown, and made her think she'd done it herself. I made her think she was mad. But when I convinced her that you were mine, Leigh, always mine, she went into the closet and hanged herself."

"And I went away," Leigh said.

"You went away. You didn't come back. You married Mari. I had to do something, didn't I? I sent the cable. You came back as I hoped you would, with Mari, of course. I had to drive her away, or destroy her. So I let her know she wasn't wanted. I did a good job on the room. I hoped . . . Oh, but Judge Sam was wise. He sent Nellie down to get me. And Amantha, and Geraldine, all that same night, lucky for me!

"But I was last! He told me he knew! Knew what? I had played at Old Dandy when I was a child. I was doing it again. And now, finally, he had begun to wonder about Wilton, about Ellen. He suspected, even more, I think, he was sure. He told me that if Old Dandy's light was seen again, he would send me away. He had completely fulfilled his responsibility to me. I didn't know what it was. He wouldn't say."

But Mari knew. Watching Fern's face change as the great gout of blood spread across her skirt, Mari knew. She thought of the ripped photograph, white shreds falling from Phoebe's fat hands; Phoebe's plump body, her round gray eyes so filled with sadness, staring unaware into the camera's recording lens.

Mari knew. Her almond eyes filled with

tears, tears of pity for a world in which sorrow never ends.

Fern's voice had grown softer, weaker. " 'Bad blood,' he said. But wouldn't say why. I knew about my parents, but I never knew who they were. I tried and tried, but Judge Sam had covered his tracks well. My tracks well, I guess. And it didn't matter. He said he would send me away. Me. And I belonged in Douglass Acres. He took me out to the balcony and said, 'Look. This is what you forfeit if you continue.' I pushed him over. I rode the dumbwaiter down, and set the candle out. Dumbwaiter, servants' staircase . . ."

She grimaced. "My tools. Made for me." She sighed. "You almost saw me, Leigh. You on the terrace where you always walked when you were troubled. And Mari, yes, Mari, at the kitchen door. But the dark, the dark."

Pink bubbles gathered at Fern's lips. "I wanted to be a Douglass, Leigh. Phoebe loved me. Phoebe." The weak voice stopped on an expelled breath. The luminous gray eyes rolled up. A strange rippling shudder moved her long, lithe body from head to toe, and when that subsided, she was dead.

Chapter 18

Later on, when they could talk, Leigh told Mari about that day. How, in the morning, he had found Judge Sam's papers disturbed. Leigh didn't know what anyone could have been looking for, but he checked all of the old files. In one, he found a newspaper clipping which told of a murder in Boston. Nineteen years before, judging by the article dateline, a man named William Poster had been murdered by his wife, who then committed suicide. A child survived. A child named Fern.

Leigh was sure that Fern Poster and Fern Carrier were one and the same. The age fit, the time Fern had come to Douglass Acres fit, too. And why else would Judge Sam have had the clipping after all those years. But Leigh took that information to Henley, to have an investigation made in Boston. Leigh asked some of the older people in Jessup if they had ever heard of William Poster. A number of them seemed to know the name, but were unwilling to talk about it.

Meanwhile, Leigh had begun to remember

bits and pieces from the past. Ellen had said, the night before she died, that he didn't want to go away from Fern. Wilton had, for years, kept telling him that Fern, though actually his cousin, was like a sister to him, and before he died, Wilton had thrown Leigh together with Ellen, always drawing Fern out of what once had been a threesome. And finally, Fern herself, the change in her, the way she had come to look so much like Ellen that Leigh had been stunned when he first saw her on the steps of Douglass Acres.

That day, waiting for Henley to have an answer to his query, he had, out of desperation, spoken to Ian. Ian, always suspicious of Leigh, had confessed that since Leigh's return Ian himself had noticed that Fern was trying to become Ellen, and soon realized that Fern was using him to make Leigh jealous.

The two men decided they must have some means of setting a trap for Fern. And that night, Mari found the gun on her pillow. Fern, taking it from Judge Sam's apartment, must have disarranged the old man's papers without noticing that, just as Leigh hadn't known the gun was gone. Fern had hoped that Leigh would send Mari away, but remain in Douglass Acres. The gun, in Mari's hands, accused her before the whole family. It was what Leigh and Ian had hoped for in a way. Leigh instantly seized that as the excuse to say he would take Mari away. They would leave together forever. He didn't dare wait. He knew he must force Fern to expose herself. For he couldn't be sure how long Mari could bear up under the strain in the house. He couldn't be sure, even, how long he himself could stand it.

Mari could see it then, as he described it. She knew that Ian hid in the drawing room. He was there when she went down to plead with Leigh while he called Boston for the charter plane.

The house finally settled into its nighttime rhythm. Leigh waited on the servants' staircase. Ian remained in the drawing room.

It was Leigh who first saw the slim, creeping shadow. He trailed it down the steps, then seized it. The shadow became a quivering old lady. Arlene, hysterical with terror. Leigh had taken her to Nellie, hoping that she would calm down, and then Phoebe had come in crying that Mari was no longer in her room. Somehow, between the patrols that Phoebe and Arlene had made, while Ian and Leigh waited, Fern had slipped out of the house, and Mari had gone after her moments later.

Ian and Leigh rushed out to the terrace. They saw Old Dandy's light at the underground room, and Fern disappearing through the door. As they crept up, they heard the gun go off, the gun that Fern must have gotten again some time before dawn.

Leigh, when he told Mari, held his voice steady. Yet she heard the horror in his careful words. He saw her, frozen to Fern, in the blazing light of the torch, while sounds of the shot echoed in the empty room . . .

All of that came later, when they could talk again.

Now they knelt beside Fern's body. Wordless, waiting.

Mari thought of the shredded photograph, of the terrible sadness in Phoebe's round gray eyes.

And Phoebe herself came down the narrow wooden steps. She felt her way along the wall to the bottom. She stumbled, panting, on the last step. She crumpled to the floor, a great heap of black, of wrinkling flesh that aged even more in seconds, and of sagging cheeks that were wet with tears. She put a fat hand on Fern's long dark hair.

"I loved you so," Phoebe whispered. She looked up at Leigh and Mari. "She always had such beautiful eyes. Her father's eyes, you know."

"Yes," Mari whispered. "I understand."

"Judge Sam took her away from me, and

gave her to poor Billy to raise. I don't suppose Billy's wife wanted her, or perhaps she didn't know the truth. But Billy took her. It was over. That's what Judge Sam said. But I must remember. So he put up that picture taken not long before Fern was born. And when Billy Poster . . . died, and his wife with him, then Judge Sam got Fern, and brought her home to us. It was our responsibility, he told me. She had my bad blood. My responsibility. He made me swear I'd never tell. He promised to send her away forever if I did. I wanted to keep her near me. I never broke my word to him. When Billy died, I went into mourning, too. Arlene, for her love, without sin, me for mine, but with sin." Phoebe bent over Fern. "But she never knew."

"She knew you loved her," Mari whispered.

"I loved her. Yes. That's why I couldn't let her do it. I never knew the whole thing, you see. Oh, about the candles when she was a child . . . yes, yes, I suspected she had to do that. But the effigy, Mari, that was when I saw . . . I saw it all then. I had to stop her. Poor child, there was only one way for it to end. Here. Now. This way." Phoebe brushed her wet cheeks. "Begun so long ago, and finished here." She raised her face. "Leigh, take Mari out into the fresh air and light. Do it now. I'll wait with Fern. I want to be alone with Fern."

Leigh tightened his arm around Mari. He led her to the steps, up them through fading gray shadows.

She became aware of a thousand small hurts, butterflies of pain fluttering around her. She felt her bloody knees and hands, her bruised cheeks, the great throbbing in her head.

But outside, a fresh breeze touched her. The sky above the distant hills was streaked with pink, and a rim of sun spilled glowing color through the brooding clouds and over the rolling meadows.

And near the door, Old Dandy's candle burned.

Amantha met them there. "My dear boy," she cried, "what is going on? Arlene and Nellie are weeping in the front driveway. Ian is shouting at the telephone. I cannot find Phoebe anywhere. Jeff is breaking bottles in the kitchen. Geraldine has packed her clothes." Amantha fluttered her silken hands. "Will we never have peace in this house?"

"I think we will," Leigh said. He knelt, blew out the candle. "Old Dandy's gone forever."

Mari whispered. "Not him. He was good, Leigh. He stood for love." And she thought, Judge Sam's demon is dead.

Leigh smiled at her, and rose. A warm, earthy quality now glowed in his face again, melting the lines from his brow, and the dark shadows from his eyes for good.

We hope you have enjoyed this Large Print book. Other Thorndike Press or Chivers Press Large Print books are available at your library or directly from the publishers. For more information about current and upcoming titles, please call or write, without obligation, to:

Thorndike Press
P.O. Box 159
Thorndike, ME 04986
USA
Tel. (800) 223-6121
(207) 948-2962
(in Maine and Canada, call collect)

OR

Chivers Press Limited
Windsor Bridge Road
Bath BA2 3AX
England
Tel. (0225) 335336

All our Large Print titles are designed for easy reading, and all our books are made to last.